"It was [illegible]
friend," Max continued. "But now, through the consciousness, I've gotten to see what life's like at home, my real home. All I can think about is getting back there. And it's not as if I can take you with me, so . . ." He shrugged. "It's just as well we're officially not together."

"What?" Liz said again. It was Max talking. She was sure of it. Whenever the consciousness was in control of him, his face was totally lifeless. But now his eyes were blinking and sparkling; his skin looked healthy. He was totally there. But how could he say these things to her?

"What?" Max mocked with a smirk. "Listen. I'll spell it out for you. I don't love you. I never did. It was fun, but it's time for me to go back where I belong."

ROSWELL HIGH

THE SALVATION

by

MELINDA METZ

POCKET BOOKS

This book is a work of fiction. Although the physical setting of the book is Roswell, New Mexico, the high school and its students, names, characters, places and incidents are either products of the author's imagination or are used fictitiously. Any resemblance to actual events or locales or persons, living or dead, is entirely coincidental.

An imprint of Simon & Schuster UK Ltd. A Viacom Company
Africa House, 64-78 Kingsway, London WC2B 6AH

Produced by 17th Street Productions, Inc.,
33 West 17th Street, New York, NY 10011

A CIP catalogue record for this book is available from the British Library

ISBN 07434 08926

1 3 5 7 9 10 8 6 4 2

Printed by Omnia Books Ltd, Glasgow
First published in USA in 1998 by Archway Paperbacks.

For Laura J. Burns—
Roswell High wouldn't be the same place
without your creativity and dedication.

ONE

Liz Ortecho stared into the open grave. At the bottom she could see Adam wrapped in the flowered sheet she'd chosen. His body looked so small down there. So lonely.

Tears blurred her vision until all she could see was a splotch of colors in the hole. Being alone was the thing Adam hated most. He'd spent years held prisoner underground by the alien-hunting agents of Project Clean Slate. The agents and guards and the doctors running the experiments on him were his only contact with the outside world.

It wasn't fair. Adam had just started to have a normal life. He'd just found people who truly cared about him. And now . . . Liz let out a shuddering breath.

Alex Manes gave her shoulder a squeeze, then stepped forward and dropped a photograph into the grave. It fluttered down to Adam's body.

"What was that?" Liz asked, wiping her eyes with the heel of her hand.

"It was a picture from the party we had at the UFO museum," Alex answered as he took a step back and stood next to her again. "Sorry you weren't in it. You weren't there that night."

"It's okay," Liz answered. "At least Adam has some company now." A piece of her long, dark hair flew over her face. She didn't bother to brush it away, but her best friend, Maria DeLuca, did it for her. Then Maria approached the grave. She took seven little vials of her aromatherapy oil out of her purse. One by one she poured drops of them into the hole. Liz caught the scent of roses, eucalyptus, cedar, ylang-ylang, cinnamon, and almonds.

Fresh tears stung her eyes as Maria poured the last vial and the odor of green leaves, new leaves, leaves just opening to the sunlight, joined the mix. Adam's scent, Liz thought. She pulled in a deep breath, smelling the perfume that filled the air every time the seven of them—she, Max Evans, Michael Guerin, Maria, Alex, Isabel Evans, and Adam—had formed a group connection.

The connection would never be the same, not without Adam's green leaf scent, without the yellow of his aura, without the note of music unique to him. Liz pulled in another deep breath, trying to memorize the perfume, trying to imprint it and make it a part of her forever.

By the time Maria moved back into place beside Liz, the scent of the oils had already begun to fade. "That was nice," Liz forced herself to say, struggling to get the words past the salty lump in her throat. Maria nodded, clearly unable to speak.

Isabel and Michael exchanged a look, then Isabel moved forward and knelt beside the grave. She whispered something, Liz couldn't hear what, then leaned down into the hole as far as she could and dropped a plastic sun next to Adam. Liz was glad Isabel had thought of that. Liz knew it was irrational, but she hated thinking of Adam being trapped underground again, separated from light and warmth by layers of the desert earth.

He's dead, she told herself. *He doesn't know where he is.*

Dead.

The word had a heavy weight in her mind. Like a stone.

It had happened so quickly, the transition from living to dead. One instant Adam was standing beside her in the hangar where Elsevan DuPris was holding the spaceship. The next instant Adam was on the ground with a hole going all the way through his body. Right through the center of his heart.

Even with Adam's form lying in the ground, it was hard for Liz to completely believe he was . . . not alive. *It should take longer,* she thought. *No one should be able to die so quickly. There should be time to realize it was happening. To do something. To say good-bye.*

Liz's eyes returned to the grave as Isabel rose gracefully to her feet. Michael immediately moved forward, touching Isabel's arm briefly as he passed her. He stared down at Adam's body for a long moment, then he opened his backpack and pulled out a shiny silver toaster.

"It's too heavy—," Liz began, hating the thought of the toaster hitting Adam's defenseless body.

It doesn't matter—he's dead, she told herself again, trying to make it real. Trying to accept it.

Michael dropped the toaster, but he must have used his power to push the molecules of oxygen closer together underneath it because it floated down into the hole as lightly as a feather.

"We got DuPris," Michael said, his voice harsh as he stared down at Adam's prone form. "He's dead. Not that that helps you any."

When she heard the name DuPris, Liz's heart practically stopped. She flashed on the vivid memory of DuPris turning toward Adam, directing the power of the Stone of Midnight at him and killing him as casually as swatting a fly. He'd done it to prove a point in an argument he was making. It was nothing personal. Adam happened to be there when DuPris wanted to make a little demonstration.

Liz's stomach cramped as she thought about how casually DuPris had annihilated Adam. Yes, DuPris was dead now. But that didn't seem like punishment enough. Not after all that he'd done—not only killing Adam, but killing Adam's parents, Max and Isabel's parents, and Michael and Trevor's parents by making their ship crash back in 1947.

"Liz," Maria said gently. "Are you ready?"

Liz realized it was her turn, her turn to try to find a way to say good-bye. Reluctantly she took the few steps that brought her to the edge of the grave.

"Adam . . ." Liz hesitated. What was there to say? What was the point of saying anything?

"Adam, I don't know what happens after we die," she said finally, trying to keep her voice from breaking. "Who knows, maybe there's a way to bend back time, or maybe you've been converted into another form of energy and you can hear me or *feel* me." Her breath started to come in hard pants as she struggled not to cry harder than she already was. She didn't want to break into the big, noisy sobs that would make it impossible for her to talk. She hadn't found the right thing to say. She couldn't lose it yet.

"If you can hear me, I just want you to know that I'm never going to forget you," Liz said, tears coating her cheeks. "Part of you is going to live in me—just the way my sister, Rosa, does. And maybe that way . . . maybe it's like you'll never have to be lonely again."

Liz opened the shopping bag she'd been cradling against her chest. She pulled out a snow globe with the Empire State Building in it. She'd bought it for herself years ago to keep her dream of moving out of Roswell to the big city alive. But now she wanted Adam to have it.

She glanced over her shoulder at Michael. "Help me?" she asked, holding up the heavy glass globe.

Michael was at her side in two long strides. Liz twisted the key in the base of the globe and the song "New York, New York" began to play. Liz nodded to Michael, then released the globe. It floated down to Adam, tiny snowflakes flurrying. "Sorry we never got to make our road trip," she whispered.

"Let's cover him up," Michael said. He took Liz's hand, then held out his other hand to Isabel. Liz reached toward Alex, and he pulled Maria over to join the group. In moments they'd formed the connection between them. It felt washed out and watered down without Adam and without Max.

Liz pushed the thought of Max aside. She couldn't think about him now. He was almost as lost to her as Adam was, and if she let her mind go there, she was afraid something inside her would snap, leaving her as limp and vacant as a rag doll.

She turned her attention to the connection, feeling the power running between them, taking comfort in the closeness of her friends' auras wrapping around her.

Michael threw out an image of Adam eating a piece of toast, looking amazed as if it was some kind of miracle. Maria shot back an image of Adam doing the alien bop. Alex added a picture of Adam intent on understanding the circuitry of an electronic device. Isabel showed them Adam taking off his sunglasses and tilting his head back to the sun. Liz answered with a picture of Adam's bright green eyes, eyes alive with wonder and hope and love.

Then together they directed the power of the connection toward the mound of earth on the far side of the hole and slowly filled in Adam's grave until it was indistinguishable from the desert around it.

Each of the two Stones of Midnight was smaller than Michael's thumbnail. They weighed almost nothing. But their presence in Michael's pocket was almost intolerable. It was like carrying around two armed nukes.

He pulled out the worn map of the United States from the little cubbyhole carved into the soft limestone wall of the cave. It was one of the few things left in there. Now that Michael lived on his own, no more a human pinball in the machine of the foster care system, he didn't spend much time at the cave. It seemed odd now that it had once been his second home.

Michael unfolded the map. He needed a place, a safe place, a place no one would think of looking for the Stones. His best bet would be to find somewhere that he had absolutely no connection to—someplace he'd never even heard of. Someplace random.

"Round and round she goes, and where she stops, nobody knows," he muttered as he closed his eyes and ran his finger in circles over the map. He tapped the paper, then opened his eyes. He'd chosen Montauk, New York, a little town at the tip of Long Island.

It was a little risky to teleport. Who knew who'd be nearby on the other end? But it would be dark on the East Coast already, and the odds of re-forming right in front of a Clean Slate agent weren't all that good. Michael focused his thoughts on a stretch of beach in Montauk, then let his molecules get slippery enough to slide away from each other, trying not to resist as his body broke apart.

When he re-formed, he found himself alone except for a big black Lab who seemed unimpressed by the amazing materializing alien. Good. Michael quickly scanned the beach. He was tempted to throw the Stones into the churning ocean, but he and his friends might need them again later. Sometimes it was good to be the ones with the nukes.

Michael scanned the beach and spotted a large rock surrounded by a group of smaller ones. He jogged over to the rocks and concentrated on the jagged, wet surface of the largest one. Concentrating hard, Michael used his mind to *shove* some of the molecules out of the way. The rock changed shape in front of his eyes as an indentation started to form. When he'd made a small but deep hole, he placed the Stones inside, then quickly *pushed* the molecules back into place.

"Safe as they're gonna get," he said. He took one glance around at the empty beach, and he was out of there.

As soon as his body had re-formed in his apartment above the UFO museum, Michael headed to the bedroom. Isabel, Maria, Liz, Alex, and Michael's brother, Trevor, were all gathered around the bed, staring down at Max's pale, motionless body.

The sight of his best friend lying there like a corpse made Michael's heart squeeze, but he tried to ignore it. It's like another friggin' funeral, Michael thought before he could stop himself.

"How is he?" he asked.

No one answered for a moment, but the group around the bed exchanged glances. "The same," Alex finally said, meeting Michael's eyes for a split second.

"It's just so awful, knowing he's in there somewhere," Maria blurted out. "It's like that story we had to read for English, Iz. You know, the one where the guy got walled up in the cellar, but he was still alive, and—"

Liz's face visibly contorted, and Maria blushed. "And . . . and I'm going to stop talking now," Maria said quickly. "Sorry. I'm upset and hence stupid."

"It's not stupid," Liz answered, her dark brown eyes intent on Max's face. "You're right. He's trapped in there, in his own body."

Michael shot a quick look at Max's face. A quick look was all he could take. Max's vacant expression and empty blue eyes sent a creeping shiver down Michael's spine.

"Does this happen to many beings who are connected to the collective consciousness?" Alex asked Trevor. He turned so that his back was to Max's face, and Michael knew he couldn't take it anymore, either.

"Yeah," Maria said, turning away from the bed as well. "You're the expert, right?" Trevor had grown up on the home planet, so he was the only one who *could* have experience with this type of thing.

Trevor took a long, deep breath, and it was all Michael could do to keep from shaking his brother to make him hurry up and talk. They had to figure out a way to help Max.

"This is extreme," Trevor admitted finally, shaking his head. He ran his fingers through his longish brown hair. "The consciousness doesn't usually do a hostile takeover like this unless there's an objective. It probably has some kind of plan, something it needs that Max can get."

Something like the Stones, Michael thought. At least he was the only one who knew where they were.

"And until they decide to use him, he'll just be—" Isabel jerked her chin toward Max's still form.

"Yeah. At least I think so," Trevor answered solemnly.

"I'm starting to feel a little like Grumpy or Doc," Alex said, scratching at the back of his head.

"What are you talking about?" Michael demanded.

"Sorry. I made a Maria," Alex said with a nervous laugh. "I just meant we're all standing here, all helpless, looking at, you know, Snow White postapple."

No one laughed. Michael couldn't take it anymore. He'd had enough of standing around staring at Max, acting like that was all they could do. He turned to his brother, crossing his arms over the front of his denim jacket.

"You want to shatter the consciousness, and we want to help," Michael said, staring his brother in the eye. "It might be the only way to free Max. So what do we do?"

Trevor walked over to the desk by the wall and leaned back against it, squeezing his eyes shut. None of which was a good sign to Michael.

"DuPris was going to have me use one of the

Stones to open a wormhole and go back home," Trevor answered slowly. "I was supposed to get a squadron together and break into the consortium chamber, then get the third Stone and bring it back to him. With all three, he could have shattered it."

"Sounds like a plan," Michael said.

"Except pretty much everyone would die in the process," Trevor said, his tone serious. "The third Stone is guarded by the greatest defensive technology ever known to our planet. There would be a lot of carnage."

"Oh," Michael said, his frustration level skyrocketing.

"I told DuPris we should find another way. I told him it was a suicide mission," Trevor said, starting to pace. "But, well, he didn't have a problem with—" He stopped and stared at the blank white wall in front of him.

"With murder," Isabel finished.

An eruption of fury exploded through Michael as he thought about what DuPris had done to Adam. But he couldn't think about that now. He couldn't bring Adam back, but he could focus on Max. Max was still alive. If you could call it that.

Michael could tell his friends were all thinking the same thing as they turned again to stare at their fallen friend.

"There's got to be another way—," Alex began.

"Wait," Liz interrupted suddenly, her eyes wide. "I'm not sure. . . ." She dropped her voice to a whisper.

"I don't think it's a good idea to be talking about this *here.*"

"You're right," Michael agreed. It was possible that the consciousness could still hear what was going on around Max even if Max wasn't actively listening. The guy could be nothing more than a radio wave transmitter at this point.

Michael led the way into the kitchen and stood behind one of the chairs that surrounded the table.

"Before we go on, there's something I have to tell you," Trevor said, standing across from Michael as the others pulled up chairs.

Michael felt another wave of trepidation rush through him. Trevor's tone had made it clear this was going to be big.

"I know you all want to help shatter the consciousness because you think it will free Max." Trevor shifted his weight uncomfortably. "That could happen. But it's more likely Max will die."

"What?" Liz spat, her voice full of panic.

"When the consciousness rips apart, the beings that form it probably aren't going to survive," Trevor continued, watching Liz carefully. "Since Max is on earth, maybe it will be different for him, but . . ."

Michael sank down into the chair in front of him. He felt like he'd been kneecapped.

"We can't," Isabel said, staring at Michael. "We can't do that to him."

Maria touched Michael's shoulder so quickly, he almost thought he'd imagined it. "We don't really have a choice, do we?" she said, glancing from Isabel to Liz. "If Max was the way he was even a few days ago—sometimes totally absorbed in his connection to the consciousness, but sometimes not—then, well, then at least he'd be able to have some kind of life. But now . . ." She let her words trail off, and a heavy silence fell over the room.

"Now he's basically dead, anyway," Isabel said tonelessly.

"Iz—," Michael began.

"No, Michael, she's right," Isabel said, holding up her chin. "Shattering the consciousness might kill Max, but it's also the only way we might be able to save him."

Her words came out sounding ice encrusted, but Michael knew her better than that. Inside, where no one could see, she was wailing and pulling out her hair. Michael knew that whatever they were going to do, they had to get it over with. None of them could live like this for very long—without knowing what was going to happen.

"So what do we do? What's the new plan?" Michael asked, ready for action.

Trevor kicked the kitchen cabinet with one heel. "I don't know," he confessed.

"Maybe there is some way we could boost the power of the two Stones we have," Alex said, leaning his arms against the table. "Maybe we don't even have to get the third one."

Isabel looked up at the clock above the stove and

stood quickly. "I can't do this now," she said. "My parents are expecting me home for dinner. It's family night. No missing it." She let out a short burst of breath, and her eyes filled with tears. "I guess I'll have to tell them Max is still working on his science project with Liz or something." Isabel shook her head back as if she was trying to keep the tears inside. "It's been three days of excuses for why he's not home now."

"Maybe I should change my face and put in an appearance as Max," Michael said. "We don't know how long it's going to take to figure out a way to shatter the consciousness. Max can't be missing in action for weeks."

"I'll do it," Trevor volunteered, stepping forward. "That way you can stay with Max."

"Really?" Michael said. Trevor confirmed with a nod. "Thanks, man. You should plan on staying there for a while. Isabel can coach you."

"Maria and I are scheduled to work tonight," Liz said. "Everyone try to come up with a plan, and we'll talk at school tomorrow."

"Good," Michael said as Isabel, Trevor, Maria, and Liz headed out.

"Want me to hang out and keep you company?" Alex asked.

Michael shook his head, stuffing his hands in his pockets. "Go. I'll see you tomorrow."

"At the risk of sounding like a feminine hygiene commercial or something, call me if you need to talk," Alex said as he left the room.

Michael continued to sit at the table, the silence wrapping around him, pressing down on him until he felt like he couldn't breathe.

"It's Max. It's still Max," he burst out. He slammed to his feet and strode to the bedroom, then sat down on the side of the bed next to Max.

"Knock, knock." Michael reached out and tapped gently on Max's forehead. "Remember how you used to love those knock-knock jokes when I first met you? Some of them were really lame. I've got to tell you, I only laughed to be polite. You know what a polite guy I am."

Max's eyes stared up at the ceiling, glassy and blank.

Michael knocked on his head again, a little harder this time. "Knock, knock." He waited a moment. "Okay, I'll answer for you—who's there?" Michael continued the joke, doing both parts himself. "Boo. Boo who? What are you crying for, you big baby?"

He brushed Max's hair off his forehead. "Remember that one?" he asked.

There was no answer.

Michael had the eerie feeling he was never going to hear Max's voice again.

TWO

"So, this is Max's room," Isabel told Trevor as she opened the door to the bedroom. "Pretty basic. Computer. Books. Clothes. Assorted Liz Ortecho memorabilia in a box in his closet he thinks I don't know about."

An arrow of pain sliced through Isabel. Max was so different from the guy who had collected all the Liz stuff. Different. Yeah, right. That made it sound like he was just going through some guy testosterone surge and acting like a jerk or something.

God, she wished that was all that was wrong with him.

"Anything else I need to know?" Trevor asked.

"Just try to act Max-like—responsible, logical, somewhat saintish, and . . . and . . ." Isabel swallowed hard. She glanced around the room, looking for something that needed straightening. Why did Max have to be so neat? She had to have something to occupy her hands, occupy her *brain*.

Isabel spun toward Max's bookshelf and started to rearrange the books by height. "I'm sure you'll be fine," she finished, eyes on her work.

"Michael told me you always clean when you get scared," Trevor commented matter-of-factly.

"I'm not scared. And Michael should keep his big mouth shut," Isabel answered automatically. She hesitated with her hand on one of the tallest books. Maybe she should be doing this by color.

"You're not scared?" Trevor asked. He leaned against the edge of the bookcase and raised an eyebrow.

"Okay, so I am," Isabel confessed. She moved her hand from the tall book to one with a red binding, then back again. Which way was better—color or size? Or maybe author? She jerked her hand toward a book by Asimov.

Trevor reached out and grabbed her by both wrists, tugging her over to the bed. He sat down and pulled her down next to him. "Talk to me," he said, his gray eyes intent on her face.

"I'm not in the mood," Isabel snapped. She couldn't believe this guy. They barely knew each other, and he was expecting her to let herself go all soft and squishy. Yes, they'd had one nice dance. Yes, he'd helped her get through her *akino* without connecting to the consciousness. But that didn't mean she was going to serve her psyche to him on a plate. That was just not her style.

She met his gaze with a challenging one of her own, waiting for him to apologize for getting all Montel on her. He just looked right back at her.

"I was afraid most of the time I was with DuPris," Trevor told her finally, breaking the silence. "Especially when I had to connect with him so we could combine powers. The stuff I saw in his head . . . I'm never going to be able to forget it."

Isabel studied him for a long moment. "How early on did you connect with him?"

"Pretty much right away," Trevor admitted.

"And you stayed with him even after you knew what he was? Even after you knew he was evil?" I *really* don't know Trevor, she thought. The guy obviously had some serious issues. How could he have stayed on as DuPris's little personal assistant, knowing the truth about him?

A faint blush crept up Trevor's throat. He ran his fingers over the redness. "This human body is way too affected by emotions."

"Answer the question," Isabel snapped.

"Yes, I stayed with him," Trevor replied. He started to rub his throat, as if he was trying to erase the blush. "I was raised to believe that sacrifice to the cause—the rebellion against the collective consciousness—was an honor. The greater the sacrifice, the greater the honor."

"That doesn't exactly explain." Isabel crossed her arms over her leather jacket and leveled him with a glare. She wasn't going to let him off the hook. This was too important.

"When I linked up with DuPris, I saw images of torture, of hideous cruelty. But DuPris said that the acts were necessary sacrifices, vital to our cause," Trevor explained. "It made me sick. But I believed nothing was more important than destroying the consciousness—no matter what it took."

He stood up and paced around the carpeted area between Max's bed and his dresser. Then he turned and faced Isabel. "I stayed with him even after I knew he killed Michael's and my parents," he blurted out. "I still didn't think DuPris was evil. Just determined. Willing to do whatever it took to end the control of the consciousness. Our parents had to be killed, or the Stone of Midnight would have been returned to the home planet and all chance of shattering the consciousness would have been lost."

Tears formed at the corners of Isabel's eyes. Trevor wasn't just talking about his parents. He was talking about her parents, too.

Trevor started talking faster. "I thought the cause was worth even that sacrifice," he said, stopping in front of her. "I thought no price was too high if it meant the consciousness would be shattered and the beings of our planet would be free again."

Isabel thought about Max. Unable to speak, unable to move unless the collective consciousness allowed it. She had risked death itself so she wouldn't have to join the consciousness and end up like her brother. She could almost understand why Trevor was willing to accept even the murder of his parents as a necessary loss.

She shifted on the bed, wiping her moist palms on the plaid comforter. "What changed your mind about DuPris?" she asked, eyeing Trevor.

"When he killed Adam," Trevor said, straightening his posture. "That was not necessary, not to shattering the consciousness, not to anything. That's when I understood the truth about DuPris."

Greasy streaks of puke green shame began snaking through Trevor's aura, along with splotches of crimson anger. Anger at himself. Isabel was sure of that.

"You killed DuPris one instant after you realized the truth," Isabel reminded him. "He was a hero to you, and you didn't hesitate to take him down. Don't forget that." A couple of the shame streaks lightened.

"Thanks," Trevor muttered. He sat back down beside her. Isabel could feel the edge of his aura brushing against hers, although their bodies weren't even touching. He's one of the good guys, she thought.

"I can't go more than a couple of minutes without thinking about Max," she said, surprising herself. She hadn't planned to go there. Isabel shot a glance at the bookcase. The desire to get up and rearrange it was like an itch in her brain, but she refused to let herself do it. She moved a little closer to Trevor instead. He didn't speak, didn't press her.

"If something happens to him . . ." She stopped and cleared her throat when she heard her voice crack. "Well, something's already happened to him. But if—I don't think I could—" She clenched a fistful of bedspread in each hand and shook her head, closing her eyes. "I just can't talk about this."

"You don't have to talk. But you don't have to go

through this alone, either. You have Michael and the others." He hesitated, then took her hands. "You have me, if that means anything."

His hands felt warm and soft around hers. "It does," she told him.

They sat there side by side in silence as the late afternoon light faded and the room grew dim and then dark. Isabel heard the front door open, then the sound of her parents' voices.

"You better change," she said. She reached over and flicked on the lamp on the nightstand. When she looked back at Trevor, his eyes had already lightened from gray to blue, his hair from brown to blond. A moment later Max was sitting beside her.

Except it wasn't really Max. It had been a long time since she'd really been with her brother.

Liz tightened her grip on the paper bag in her hand as she climbed up the steps to Michael's apartment. He opened the door before she had a chance to knock. "I thought I'd visit Max before school."

"You want company?" Michael asked.

"No, I'm good," Liz said. Michael stepped back to let her inside.

"I'm going to head out, then. I want to make a stop at the doughnut place," he said, hand on the doorknob.

"Yeah, go, it's fine," she assured him, trying to act casual. "I'll lock up when I leave." As soon as the door closed, Liz hurried through the living room and down the hall to the bedroom. She took a moment to brace herself for the sight of Max's lifeless face, then stepped inside.

"Um, I made you some of those blueberry-and-jalapeño muffins you like," she announced, her voice coming out too loud and phony. "I'll just leave them on the dresser. I guess the consciousness will let you eat sometime."

Just to keep you alive in case it needs to use you for something, she added silently. She sat down gingerly on the side of the bed and gazed down at Max, forcing herself not to turn away at the sight of his slack mouth and dull eyes.

"I know you're in there somewhere, Max," she said. "I'm just going to assume you can hear me." Now what? Liz tilted her head from side to side, the bones in her neck cracking slightly. "So let me tell you what's been going on. Elsevan DuPris is dead, so you don't have to worry about that. I know how much you worry about things. We're all safe. No crisis."

Except the crisis involving Max himself. She pushed away the thought and continued. "I do have some sad news about Adam. He's dead, Max." She struggled to control the tremor that had infected her voice. "DuPris killed him."

Liz checked Max's eyes. Not a flicker of emotion or even awareness.

"I don't know if you ever noticed that Adam had a crush on me. And when you—when you weren't around that much, I started spending more time with him. He made me feel good. Special, you know?"

Tears burned her eyes as she remembered the time she spent with Adam. She twisted her hair into a knot, then let it fall back down her back, trying to keep her composure. It wasn't going to help Max if she sat here sobbing.

"I don't know why I'm even telling you this," she said. "No, that's not true," she corrected herself. "I'm telling you because I want you to know that although I really cared about Adam, I never fell in love with him. I've never loved anybody but you, Max. I don't think I ever will."

Liz did another eye check. Nothing.

"You might find it hard to accept that," she continued, wanting to believe he was listening and praying he could. "I know I broke up with you. But that's because you were so deeply connected to the consciousness that you weren't even you anymore. The way I felt . . . the way I feel—it hasn't changed. I love you. I love you so much."

She reached out and ran her fingers down his cheek. His skin felt warm and dry, but a chill ran through her.

"I should go. School." Liz stood up. "I'll come back later." She started for the door, then turned back, her breath coming in quick bursts. "We all heard you when you told us you were trapped that day in the hangar. We all heard you ask for help. I promise that we're going to find a way to bring you back."

A gasp escaped her lips as she did one last eye check. Max's gaze met hers directly, his eyes bright with life.

He sat up, then swung himself out of bed and

strode over to her, his eyes never leaving hers. Liz almost fell into his arms, but then he started talking, and his words made her freeze.

"I was relieved that you broke up with me," he told her. "It saved me the hassle of trying to come up with something to say to you."

"What?" Liz took an involuntary step backward and smacked into the door, the knob digging into her spine.

"It was fun for a while—having a human girlfriend," he continued. "But now, through the consciousness, I've gotten to see what life's like at home, my real home. All I can think about is getting back there. And it's not as if I can take you with me, so . . ." He shrugged. "It's just as well we're officially not together."

"What?" Liz said again. It was Max talking. She was sure of it. Whenever the consciousness was in control of him, his face was totally lifeless. But now his eyes were blinking and sparkling; his skin looked healthy. He was totally there. But how could he say these things to her?

"What?" Max mocked with a smirk. "Listen. I'll spell it out for you. I don't love you. I never did. It was fun, but it's time for me to go back where I belong. I need the Stones. With them I can open a wormhole for the return trip."

"You never loved me?" The words felt edged with razor blades as they came out of her mouth. She was almost surprised not to feel blood on her lips.

"I. Never. Loved. You. Did I say it slowly enough for you to understand that time?" he asked. He was so close to her, she could feel his breath against her forehead as he spoke, smell the familiar Max smell of his body, see the subtle flecks of a deeper blue in his light blue eyes. Everything about him was so familiar. But it was as if he were a complete stranger.

"You're lying," she said, determination settling over her face. "I don't know why, but you're lying. Are you trying to protect me from something? Because I know that you love me. There was no way you could have been pretending. I would have felt it."

Max laughed, shaking his head as if she were a child. "There are a lot of girls who've said exactly those words to a lot of guys. What makes you think you're any smarter? Now, tell me where the Stones are, and I'll be out of your way."

Slowly Liz's brain regained some of its ability to function. The Stones. This was about the Stones. He'd said it twice now.

She narrowed her eyes and studied him. Yes, he looked awake, but she'd never seen his eyes so hard or his jaw so tight before. This wasn't Max standing in front of her, not really. It was the consciousness. The consciousness was trying to manipulate her emotions to get her to reveal the location of the Stones.

Liz was half relieved, half disgusted.

"I don't know where they are," she answered. Which was true. Not that she would have told the consciousness where to find them if she had.

"If you're thinking that you can change the way I feel about you by keeping me around, you're wrong," Max said harshly. "The longer I'm with you, the more clear it is to me that we could never have been anything more than short-term. My abilities, my capacities are so beyond yours that I'd never be satisfied by you."

It's not Max, she told herself. It's not him. But the words cut her to the bone.

"Tell me where the Stones are, Liz," Max pressed.

The sound of her name on his, no, *its*, lips sent a shudder through her. "I don't know!" she screamed.

Then the Max thing blinked and crumpled to the floor, lifeless.

Max fought against the ocean of auras above him. He had to break to the surface. He had to get to Liz.

But he wasn't strong enough. The auras bore down on him with the pressure of billions of gallons of water, pushing him deeper and deeper into the consciousness, farther and farther away from Liz.

"Liz!" he screamed with his mind. "Liz!"

But there could be no answer.

Max shot images out at the closest beings, images of pain and violation, trying to express how it felt for his body and brain to be used without his consent.

He felt some flickers of sympathy from the most distant beings. Clearly he was being kept away from any that might be tempted to help him. Then an image filled his mind—a picture of him using one of the Stones of Midnight to open a wormhole and return both Stones to his home planet. This image was immediately followed by another one—Liz's stricken face.

The image of Liz multiplied, each vision of her a knife slicing through his soul. The message was clear. Either Max returned the Stones to the home planet, or he would be made to hurt those he loved again and again.

Max let out a howl of fury. He hurled himself at the auras above him, using every ounce of energy and determination to fight his way through. He had to get out, find Liz, tell her he was sorry, tell her he loved her until his throat was raw.

But there were too many of them. Billions to his one. When they slammed him back down, he didn't bother trying to get up again.

THREE

Alex snapped his combination lock shut and headed down the hall. Whatever transformation had happened to him in the wormhole hadn't worn off. He was still getting looks from every girl he passed, looks that made him feel edible or something. It was kinda freaky. And very cool.

He caught sight of Maria turning the corner. She smiled when she saw him, and when she got closer, she started to fan her face.

"I don't know what it is," she said in a breathy voice. "Whenever I'm near you, I just turn all hot and swoony." Her eyelashes fluttered, and she dropped into a half faint.

"I'll have to start carrying those, whatdoyoucallems," Alex said as he caught her by the shoulders and pushed her upright. "Smelling salts."

Maria giggled and smoothed her blond curls behind her ears. "You better. Otherwise you're going to start getting sued by hundreds of girls who injure themselves fainting at your feet."

Cracking a grin, Alex crooked his arm around Maria's neck. "I want you to know that even though I'm a babe and everything, you're not going to have to slap me around again," he said, growing serious. "Anything that needs to be done to shatter the consciousness, I'm there."

Alex was still a little embarrassed by the way he'd abandoned the group when they were gearing up to go head-to-head with DuPris. He'd gotten so caught up with his newfound babe-magnet status, he'd forgotten what was important. At least until Maria had pulled him out of a theater in the middle of a date and reminded him.

"I know that," Maria said, looking him directly in the eye. "We all know that. Hey, everyone's entitled to an occasional screwup." She shrugged, lifting her hands. "If I'd suddenly become a sex goddess, I'm sure I would have been as big an idiot as you were."

"Gee, thanks," Alex replied. Arlene Bluth winked at him as she headed by. Alex winked back. *Winked*. Who did that?

"I didn't mean that in a bad way," Maria said in a rush. "Why not take advantage of what life gives you? I mean, life is short. Very short."

"Uh-huh," Alex said, trying not to laugh as Maria babbled.

"Unbelievably short. Like that." She tried to snap her fingers and failed. "Too much moisturizer," she muttered. "Anyway, you know what I mean. Short."

Her voice was starting to tremble, and her blue eyes were shiny with unshed tears. Whoa. Talk about going from zero to sixty in three seconds.

"Short, yeah," Alex answered, deciding that agreeing was a good strategy. "But Maria, you're only sixteen. I mean—"

"And how old was Adam?" she exclaimed, her voice getting shrill. "For him life isn't even short. It's over."

Alex's stomach turned as he flashed on the memory of DuPris taking Adam down. Poor Adam. That's what this was about.

Alex took Maria by the arm and led her into the stairwell. She was about to lose it, and there was no reason for her to have to do it in public.

"What happened to Adam was horrible," Alex said quickly, trying to get Maria to listen to him before she entered the totally incoherent stage. He held both her wrists and tried to make his voice sound soothing. "But Maria, that doesn't happen to—"

"Liz's sister died," Maria interrupted, seeming to grow smaller in front of him. "People our age die all the time. It's not just Adam."

"But—"

"I used to think there was all this time," Maria said, a tear spilling over. "Huge amounts of time. I even thought you could control time with your mind—how stupid is that? I thought if you concentrated, you could stretch one minute out forever—see the tennis ball slowly coming toward the racket, you know?"

Actually, Alex didn't, but he let her go on. Maybe venting would help. Besides, interrupting hadn't worked so far.

"But now I know that you can't control time. Time controls you," she babbled, tears trembling on her eyelashes now. "And there are so many things I want to do. God, so many things."

Alex shoved his hands into his pockets and felt around. He didn't have a tissue or anything, of course. He ripped a sheet of blank paper out of his binder and handed it to Maria. He figured it was better than nothing, but she crumpled it up in her fist and kept on talking.

"It's so stupid to want things," she continued, looking around her like the answers were on the crappy concrete walls. "Or make plans. Or—"

"Wait. Hold up," Alex said, firmly this time. "Go back to the part about the things you want to do. Tell me some of them."

If he could get her to actually say something specific, he might be able to turn this around. Whatever it was she wanted to do, he'd help her do it. Start her own aromatherapy business or track down Brad Pitt so she could kiss him just once. Whatever it was, he'd probably only have to work on it for a couple of days. He loved Maria, but the girl did have sort of a short attention span. She'd forget about her mission the second another animal hit the endangered list.

Maria leaned against the dusty wall and slid down to the floor, arms wrapped around her knees. "There's no point in telling you," she said.

"Come on. I'll be your best friend," Alex teased. He sat down next to her, pulling his long sweatshirt down to cover the butt of his baggy pants. "Whatever it is you want, I'll help you figure out how to get it."

She snorted and covered her eyes with her hands. "You can't," she answered. "I've been waiting, and waiting, and waiting . . . and Michael still doesn't love me. At least he doesn't *love* love me. And I just don't know if I'm going to live long enough for him to actually figure out that . . . that . . . he *should.* That no one else is ever going to care about him as much as I do." Tears coated her cheeks and hands, and there were little smudges of makeup under her eyes. "Even if we both live to be a hundred, I don't think he's going to get it."

She pressed her forehead against her knees. Alex stared helplessly down at her crazy curls, his heart going out to his friend. This was way out of his league. He'd known she had a thing for Michael, but he hadn't realized that she had fallen heart and soul for the guy.

"If he doesn't get it, then he's a fool," Alex told her, putting his hand on her back.

Maria snorted a laugh. "Unfortunately we both know that's exactly what he is."

Liz's heart gave a little flutter as Trevor sat down across from her at the cafeteria table. She wasn't fooled into thinking he was actually Max, but it still affected her to see him.

"How's it going?" she asked, trying not to look at him. "Any trouble?"

"Nope," Trevor said, sliding his cafeteria tray into

place in front of him. "Isabel told me Max is pretty quiet in class, doesn't really volunteer, but knows the right answer if he's called on. The information the Kindred gave me to study before I came here covered way more than what I needed to know to be a good high school student."

"I bet," Liz answered, looking past him at the door to the hallway. She was relieved when she spotted Maria, Alex, and Isabel coming toward them. Talking to Trevor one-on-one would be no problem if he looked like Trevor, but it was too painful this way. Every time she glanced at him, she was slammed by the memory of her encounter with Max that morning.

Not Max, she reminded herself. The consciousness.

"What's shakin'?" Alex asked hypercheerfully, clearly having appointed himself group morale booster. He sat down on one side of her, and Maria sat down on the other, Isabel sliding onto the bench next to Trevor.

"There's something I need to tell you guys, but I want to wait for Michael to get here," Liz said, playing with the cap on her water bottle.

"You're going to cut an album and you want us to sing backup?" Alex joked. But his voice had gone down several points on the cheerometer, and Liz knew that *he* knew her news was of the not-good kind.

"He's coming," Isabel said, lifting her chin in the direction of the food line, where Michael was just accepting his change. She carefully spread a layer of grape jelly on her turkey sandwich, then added dollops of ketchup. Her blue eyes were focused on the sandwich as if it was the most important thing in her life. Clearly she'd picked up on the not-good vibe, too.

"Liz has something to tell us," Maria blurted out before Michael's butt got all the way into the seat next to Isabel's.

"What now?" Michael said, sounding resigned.

"When I was visiting Max this morning, he woke up," Liz said.

"What?" Isabel said, her eyebrows shooting up.

"Wait," Liz said, lifting her hands before Isabel could get *too* excited. "At least I thought it was him. Then I realized he was being completely controlled by the consciousness."

"How?" Isabel demanded. She picked up her sandwich, then put it back down as if she couldn't remember what it was for.

"He said some un-Max-like stuff," Liz answered, avoiding Isabel's gaze. She didn't want to go into it. In fact, she wanted to forget that it had ever happened. Not that that was possible. His words—*its* words—were seared into the flesh of her brain. "The consciousness wants Max to return the Stones. I don't think it's going to give up until it gets them."

Michael and Trevor exchanged a glance that sent a chill down Liz's spine.

"If the Stones are returned to the home planet, it's over," Trevor said with a serious doomsday tone. "Without them we have no chance of shattering the consciousness."

"Then we have to keep Max from finding them,"

Alex said, rubbing his hands together. "Simple, right?"

"Yeah, but you haven't seen what Max can do when the consciousness has control of him," Liz said, her stomach feeling as heavy as lead as she remembered how consciousness Max had once brutally attacked DuPris. "He's . . . dangerous."

Isabel dropped her head into her hands, and Liz immediately wished she hadn't said anything. She knew it was hard for Isabel to hear everyone talk about her brother like this. But it was all, unfortunately, true. And it wasn't Max's fault.

"Then we need two teams," Alex said as he leaned back in his chair. "One team will keep working on a way to annihilate the consciousness, and the other . . ."

"The other can hang with Max and take him on a wild-goose chase," Maria finished, perking up slightly. "We can make the consciousness believe we want to help it find the Stones and keep it distracted."

"We are so on the same wavelength," Alex said, crunching into a nacho.

"Huh. Go figure," Michael said, rubbing his chin.

"What?" Alex asked, his brow scrunching up.

"You two came up with a good plan," Michael deadpanned. "Didn't think it was possible."

"Oh, very funny," Maria said.

"I'll be on the distract-the-consciousness team," Liz volunteered, raising her hand to shoulder level.

"I've got to be on the other one," Trevor said, leaning his elbows on the table. "No way would the consciousness accept that I'd be willing to give it the Stones." He took a sip of his Lime Warp and grimaced.

Michael tossed him a couple of packets of hot sauce. "I'll work with you on trying to figure out what we can do with the two Stones we have."

"Just give me a chance to sew some sequins on a leotard, and you can call me your lovely assistant," Maria volunteered. She glanced at Liz. "Unless you want to switch," she said. "I get the feeling the consciousness wasn't exactly, um, *nice* to you."

Best-friend telepathy. It almost never fails, Liz thought. "Thanks. But I keep thinking about that day in the hangar, when Max was Max again, totally Max, just for those few seconds. If that happens again, I want to be there."

God, did she want to be there. She needed something from the real Max to make her stop thinking about what had happened that morning.

"I do, too," Isabel said quickly. Liz knew that the two of them were thinking exactly the same thing—please, please, please let me have one real moment with Max.

"So, Michael's the only one who knows where the Stones are, huh?" Trevor asked Maria. They sat side by side on the hood of Michael's big old Cadillac, waiting for him to teleport back to the desert so they could get to work.

"Yeah, I guess he figured it was safer that way,"

Maria answered, coughing as the wind kicked up a sand cloud all around them.

At least it's nothing personal, Trevor thought. It's not as if Michael told everyone except me. Although Trevor wouldn't be surprised if that's how it had gone down. He knew helping kill DuPris had gone a long way toward winning back Michael's trust. But he wasn't sure if his brother had gotten over the fact that Trevor had used their relationship to try to get close enough to one of the Stones so he could bring it to DuPris, back when Trevor still thought DuPris was almost a god.

"You look like him, you know?" Maria commented, leaning back a little so she could study his face. "Same eyes. Same hands. Same basic build. You even have some of the same expressions—like the raising-one-eyebrow thing."

Trevor raised one eyebrow at her, and she smiled. "Looking like him, that seems to be a good thing by earth standards."

"Oh yeah," Maria said. Then a faint blush colored her cheeks. Trevor always noticed stuff like that—blushes, teary eyes, rapid breathing. The way the human body responded to emotion fascinated him, although the sensations could be almost creepy when he felt them happening to himself. "I think I see him coming back," she added, jerking her chin toward a mesquite bush.

"You're right," Trevor agreed. He could see a network of veins forming. Blood began to rush through them, then muscle and bone began appearing, followed by the internal organs until Michael's body was whole again except for two empty eye sockets.

"This is the part that makes me *eww,*" Maria confessed, shuddering slightly as she squeezed her eyes shut.

"Something about me makes you *eww?*" Michael asked as his gray eyes solidified.

"Many things," Maria answered, peeking to make sure Michael was all intact.

Why don't I believe that? Trevor thought, catching the little swirls of pleasure that had appeared in Maria's aura as Michael teased her.

"So I have the Stones. Now what do we do?" Michael asked, slapping his hands against his dusty jeans.

Trevor shrugged. "Basically we're trying to find a way to boost their power," he answered. "But I have no idea how."

"Maybe we could each hold a Stone and then connect, and see if the two Stones are more powerful when they're linked through the connection," Michael suggested.

"First you'd have to see how powerful they are when you use them together *unconnected,*" Maria said. She slid off the hood and grinned. "Hey, I sounded like Liz for a second. Go, science girl."

She's so adorable, Trevor thought. So bouncy. Bouncy hair, bouncy personality. He shot a glance at his brother. What was the guy's problem? Didn't he notice how attractive Maria was?

"Maybe we should whip up some kind of weather

thing," Michael suggested, looking around the empty desert. "It's not like many people come out here, but just in case someone noticed, at least there would be a natural explanation."

"Sounds good to me," Trevor answered, hopping off the car.

"Your lovely assistant, Maria, agrees," Maria said with a little curtsy.

"I'll go first." Michael pulled one of the Stones out of his pocket. It began to glow with a purple-green light, a light that intensified every second. He stretched out his hand, aiming the Stone away from them.

The desert sand began to swirl, forming a tall column. The column began to whirl, dragging more sand into it.

"I don't know if this was such a good idea," Maria shouted as a large boulder got sucked into the tornado.

The funnel of spinning sand expanded. Trevor felt it sucking the ground out from under his feet, greedy for even more mass.

"Michael! The car!" Maria cried, panicked.

Trevor jerked around just in time to see the Cadillac fly into the air and whip into the funnel. Shielding his eyes with one hand, he staggered over to Maria and grabbed her wrist. Images of a man's face, a chocolate cake, and a piece of wood with a wicked-looking nail in it flashed through his mind as he made the connection. He used his powers to make both their bodies heavier, anchoring them to the ground.

Maria's hair slashed into his face, each strand like a wire whip in the furious wind. He could see her screaming something, but he couldn't hear a word.

He tilted back his head, craning to see the top of the tornado's funnel. He couldn't. But he could see the car. It was so high up, it looked like a toy.

Slowly, slowly, the car became larger, large enough for a kid to squeeze in. It's coming back down, Trevor realized. The howling wind grew a little quieter. The Cadillac touched down with a shuddering thump, and a flood of sand fell from the sky, burying Trevor, Maria, and Michael up to their knees.

Michael turned toward them, covered in grainy silt. "I didn't even use a quarter of the potential power," he told them, his eyes stunned. "I don't know what I was thinking. One of these babies opened a wormhole. This was no kind of test."

"But I bet it got people's attention," Maria said, struggling to free herself.

Trevor realized that her body—and his—was still weighted down. He used his powers again, restoring them to their usual weight and density, then he helped Maria out of the sand.

"You're right," Michael told Maria, tousling his hair and causing streams of sand to fly everywhere. "We better get out of here. We can figure out a better test tomorrow." He used the Stone to move the car over to a section of sand that was still firmly packed, then tossed the keys to Maria. "I've got to put the

Stones back. You can take the car and leave it at your place. I'll pick it up later."

"I live to serve," she muttered, twirling the keys once around her finger.

Michael turned to Trevor. "Want to come with me?" he asked.

Trevor nodded, getting the unspoken message. Michael had decided to give him another chance by letting him in on the Stones' hiding place. His brother was offering Trevor his trust for the second time. And Trevor was going to make very sure Michael didn't regret it.

FOUR

Isabel didn't want to step into the bedroom. If she did, she might end up having to use her power on Max. Well, on the consciousness, really. But she couldn't attack the consciousness without damaging Max. And even thinking about hurting her brother set the contents of her stomach agitating.

"So, are my two starlets ready to perform?" Alex asked, putting one hand on her shoulder and one on Liz's.

"Starlet? Did I actually hear you use the word *starlet?*" Isabel muttered, tossing her long, blond hair over her shoulder in an attempt to look nonchalant. "Are you from planet 1950 or what?"

But did it feel good to have Alex making dorky comments? Did it feel good to feel the warmth of his hand through her shirt? Yes, she had to admit it did. Anything calming and familiar was good at this point.

"Isabel's right," Liz jumped in. "The word you'd be wanting to use is *actor.*"

"Not actress?" Alex asked, green eyes widening in what Isabel suspected was mock surprise.

"There's no reason for a word like that to be sex differentiated," Liz said with a little nod. "No one says doctress, right?"

"Or lawyeress," Isabel added. She shot a glance at the closed bedroom door, then immediately looked away. Could it possibly be more obvious that they were all avoiding going inside?

"But then, there *is* stewardess," Alex countered, tightening his grip on her shoulder slightly.

"Flight attendant, cave boy," Isabel shot back, leveling him with a glare. She knew she should be reaching for the door handle, but she didn't. She just couldn't make her fingers go there.

"So if I want to be politically correct, I should just call all three of us chickens for standing out here having a fake argument instead of going in?" Alex asked.

"Exactly," Liz told him. She clicked her teeth together nervously, then reached out and jerked open the door.

Now that it was open, there was really no choice but to walk through, so Isabel took the plunge. There was a lot that scared her in this world, but there wasn't much she'd admit to being scared of. Once she was inside, Liz and Alex tentatively followed.

"Max, we talked it over, and we want to help you get the Stones of Midnight," Isabel blurted out almost the second she was across the threshold. She wasn't usually a blurter, but she couldn't help herself.

"I told her—everyone—how you felt, how you want to go home," Liz said, walking over to stand next to the bed. "Alex and Isabel and I decided that if that's really how you feel, we should . . . should help." She sounded scared, and Isabel noticed her eyes darting everywhere—everywhere except Max's face.

And why did I notice that? she asked herself. Answer: Because I'm looking at Liz to avoid looking at Max. She took a step closer to the bed, leaned forward, and forced herself to stare unblinkingly into her brother's empty eyes. After a moment her own eyes began to sting, but she didn't allow them to close. She kept staring, hoping for some glint, some flicker, some tiny sign that Max was in there. That he knew she was standing almost close enough to touch.

Nothing. All she saw was the light blue of his irises. The deep black circles of his pupils.

"So, Max, buddy, does that sound good?" Alex asked, lightly punching Max's shoulder. "We'll get our butts in gear and start tracking down the Stones, okay?"

Max pulled a slow, even breath. Let it out.

"We'll take that as a yes," Alex said quickly. He was so jumpy, he was practically coming out of his skin. Isabel could feel it. "We'll get right on it. And we'll report back," he added, turning toward the door.

Isabel hesitated for a second, still wanting something from Max. Then, realizing she wasn't going to get it, she started after Alex. "Aren't you coming, Liz?" she asked over her shoulder.

"I want to stay a little while," Liz answered. She had yet to look at Max. Isabel wondered why she'd want to stay, but she knew better than to ask. Liz would probably make up an answer, anyway. Isabel walked up to Liz and leaned in to whisper in her ear. "I'll leave the door open so we'll hear you if you . . . need anything."

“’Kay,” Liz whispered.

“Don’t get too close, all right?” Isabel said quietly.

“’Kay,” Liz repeated. She was almost as catatonic as Max.

Isabel walked out and trailed Alex down the hall and into the kitchen. She could hardly believe she’d just told Liz Ortecho not to get too close to Max because Isabel was afraid *Max* might hurt *Liz*. It hadn’t even been a year since Isabel was warning Max to stay away from Liz, terrified that Liz would tell their secret and get them shipped off to some alien autopsy lab.

“I was wrong about that,” she mumbled.

“Wait. What? Did I just hear you say that you were wrong about something?” Alex exclaimed, back in the hyper zone. “Has the world spun off its axis? Has gravity reversed itself? Has—”

“Your rah-rah-boy act is getting old, Alex,” Isabel informed him, immediately starting to rearrange the cereal boxes on the counter. “You don’t have to attempt to keep everyone all chipper.”

“Attempt,” Alex repeated. He slumped down in the closest chair. “Thanks a lot.”

Isabel dropped what she was doing and slid into the seat next to him.

“Look,” Isabel said, staring at the cracked surface of the table. “It would be impossible for *anyone* to make us feel better right now.”

“Yeah,” Alex agreed. He scraped a marshmallow cereal rocket off the kitchen table, turned it over in his fingers, then absentmindedly popped it into his mouth.

Isabel struggled not to look disgusted. "Do you really want to know what I was wrong about?" she asked, leaning back in her chair and letting her hair spill down behind her.

"Definitely." Alex spotted another gummy marsh-mallow and reached for it. Isabel pressed her hand over his, stopping him. Alex stared at their hands as if they were completely riveting.

"I was wrong about Liz," Isabel said, focused on their hands as well. "After Max healed her, I was sure she'd betray him, betray all of us. But she didn't. Whatever the opposite of betray is, that's what she did," Isabel added. "You and Maria, too. I was so wrong about all of you."

"I, on the other hand, knew you were a goddess the moment I first saw you," Alex said, slowly pulling his hand away. "And I wasn't wrong." He smiled sheepishly at her, then looked away.

Isabel snorted and started picking at her nails. "Have you had some kind of seizure recently?" she asked. "Something that might have caused massive memory loss? How could you possibly still have me on a pedestal after everything I've done to you?"

Like breaking up with him with all the finesse of a meat cleaver. Like pushing him away when he tried to warn her how dangerous Nikolas was. Like so, so many times just not appreciating him enough—acting like anything he did for her was simply what she deserved.

"Who said anything about a pedestal?" Alex asked. "I'm talking goddess like Greek mythology. Goddesses who were more beautiful than any mortal." He gave a grin that was half embarrassed. "But who were also strong and smart and who would do things like turn men into ashes if they felt like it."

"And that's me?" Isabel asked, not totally hating the description.

"That's you, baby," Alex said. His words were teasing, but his tone wasn't. He really meant it. He thought she was a goddess.

Isabel tilted her head and looked at him, really looked at him.

"Do I have something in my teeth?" Alex asked. He started using his finger as a toothbrush.

"No, I was just trying to decide what you are," Isabel admitted. "If I'm a goddess, then you're . . . you're like one of the guys out of a fairy tale."

"I don't think I'm liking where this is going," Alex said, sitting up straight in his chair. "You're a goddess, and I'm, what? Hansel?"

"Sort of. You're . . ." She hesitated a moment, trying to come up with the right word. "You're resourceful. Like when the witch wanted to see if Hansel was fattened up enough to eat and he kept letting her feel the chicken bone instead of his finger—that's something you would do. You think fast."

"But Hansel," Alex scoffed, throwing out his hands. "Just the name. Hansel! How lame."

Isabel shook her head and laughed. It sounded

odd, but good. "Forget Hansel. Forget fairy tales. How about Superman?" Alex brightened at this suggestion, and she grinned. "You're a good guy like he is. And you have that sort of geeky-yet-cute exterior—well, until lately, when you became a stud. Plus in the right situation you can kick some major butt."

Alex rocked his chair back on two legs. "Superman. I like it." For one second everything was fine. Then Alex glanced over his shoulder, Isabel followed his eyes, and she remembered what was going on. The smile fell from her face as Alex let the chair legs fall back to the floor with a thud.

"Think I should check on Liz?" he said.

"It's still quiet back there," Isabel answered. "Let's give her another couple of minutes. If Max—if the consciousness—bought our story, she should be safe."

"I wonder how the B team is doing," Alex said. He reached across the table, going for the marshmallow rocket again.

"Me too," Isabel agreed, letting him eat the repulsive thing without comment. Sometimes Alex just had to be Alex. And that, at least most of the time, was a very good thing.

"It sucks being the lovely assistant," Maria muttered as she maneuvered Michael's big old Caddy onto Main Street. "Trevor and Michael are off . . . someplace, probably someplace really cool. And did they even think about inviting me? Oh no. No, no. I get to drive the car back home."

She slowed down as she passed the UFO museum. She could just drop the Cadillac there and save Michael a trip. Buses ran pretty often at this time of night, so it wouldn't be too much of a pain.

But that wasn't going to happen. Maria pressed her foot on the accelerator and sped around the corner. Michael had said he'd pick up the car, and that's what he'd have to do. And if she just happened to see him through the window when he came to get it, and then just happened to wander outside, and then just happened to throw herself on the hood of the car and scream, "Kiss me, you wild Michael beast," and then just . . .

And then just happened to watch Michael run like he was training for the Olympics, she thought, rolling her eyes. Which was obviously what he would do.

Maria tried to keep her mind on the road the rest of the way home. She only ended up driving by Braille a couple of times. That's what her brother, Kevin, called it when she let the car wander a little too far to the left and started going over the little bumps marking the white divider lane—driving by Braille.

It took only two tries for her to pull the boat of a car into the driveway. Two tries and one slightly dented antenna. Hey, if Michael had a problem with it, he could do the driving himself.

Maria cut the engine and reached for the door handle, then hesitated. Being in the car was sort of like being a little tiny doll or an elf and living inside Michael's pocket. The interior actually smelled like him—all spicy-musky, with a hint of sweet-and-spicy that came from the number of crullers with hot sauce he'd consumed sitting right where Maria was now. She pulled in a deep breath and let it out with a long, content sigh.

"I have so lost it," she whispered. But she didn't get out of the car. She leaned her head back against the seat and took another breath, savoring the smell, then clicked on the radio and did a pass through the stations Michael had programmed in. She smiled when she caught a snatch of an Elvis tune. She was sure Michael had chosen that station in honor of Ray Iburg, who'd given Michael the car. Any station that played the King would have been fine by Ray.

She punched the buttons again until she found a song that matched her mood, kind of slow and sad and dreamy. She closed her eyes and let herself drift into la-la-la land, which was what she called the place in her head that was in charge of producing fantasies. That little corner of her mind was fully stocked with images of Michael. Maria picked one—Michael in a soft gray T-shirt that matched his eyes—and began to dance with it, breathing in the Michael scent, trying to make the fantasy a little more real.

"Wow." Trevor watched the waves roll into the shore again and again. Michael watched him watch, then returned his own gaze to the ocean.

"Before I hid the Stones out here, I'd been to the beach only once before, with the Evanses," Michael said. "Totally blew me away. One of the best times ever."

"I can imagine," Trevor answered, never taking his eyes from the water. "Can we go in?"

"We'd freeze," Michael replied. For the last fifteen minutes he'd been sitting here, trying to play it cool and not pull his jacket tighter around himself to fight off the wind. "If we had wet suits, we'd be okay, but—"

Trevor turned to look at Michael, and he was grinning. "We have something better," he said, pulling one of the Stones out of his pocket.

Michael smiled. He yanked off his jacket and was out of his shirt in seconds. "What are we waiting for?" he said as he shoved off his sneakers without bothering to untie them. "Last one in is a rotten egg!"

He raced across the deserted beach, aiming his Stone at the water. Trevor was right behind him. "A rotten egg? Ooh. That really hurts," he shouted.

"You ever smelled a rotten egg?" Michael yelled back. He plunged straight into the ocean and kept running, as well as he could run against the tide, until the water was chest high. "This is awesome. It's warmer than a bathtub." He spread open his arms and let himself fall backward, submerging completely. When he came back up, the first thing he saw through the salt stinging his eyes was Trevor blowing a stream of water out of his nose and coughing.

"Didn't the materials the Kindred gave you mention that the human body can't breathe underwater?" Michael asked.

Trevor answered by using both hands to splash Michael. Michael retaliated, using a little power, nothing anyone would notice, to bring a wave down on Trevor's head.

A second later Michael was kissing sand. "Truce, okay? Truce?" he called when he resurfaced.

"Okay," Trevor answered, slicking his brown hair away from his face.

"Suck-er." Michael used his power to knock Trevor on his butt. And the water war was on again.

One attack, one counterattack, one counter-counterattack, two fake truces, and one real truce later Michael stretched out on his back, allowing the warm water to support him. He couldn't stop a smile from spreading across his face. Him and his brother at the beach. It was too cool.

"I'm gonna have to build me one of these when I get back home," Trevor announced as he floated beside Michael. "After we shatter the consciousness and I help rebuild the planet, it's on the top of my list."

"Ambitious much?" Michael asked. The stars had come out, and he stared up at them, feeling like he was floating in the sky, too.

"It's going to be a big job," Trevor answered, his voice serious now. "The consciousness has been the foundation of our society for thousands of years. Together we're all going to have to figure out what we want to replace it. Sometimes I don't think the members of the Kindred think about that part enough."

"But you do." Michael glanced at his brother as

well as he could without tipping himself over.

"Yeah. I do. A system a little like the one you have in the United States might even work." Trevor flipped over on his stomach and paddled out to a sandbar just breaking through the water. He sat on it, letting the ocean advance and retreat around him.

Michael swam over and joined him. Trevor kept his eyes focused back on the beach, and Michael could feel that his brother had something big on his mind. Maybe even bigger than the consciousness, if that was possible.

"I was hoping, or wondering, I guess, if you'd come back with me when we've figured out how to break the consciousness," Trevor said finally. Michael felt an excited tingle run all over his body, but oddly, it disappeared rather quickly. "The planet is going to change forever. I want to be a part of that change." He turned toward Michael. "I want you to be a part of it, too."

"Go back home," Michael said, stating the obvious because he didn't know what else to say. He'd been dreaming about this moment for years—ever since he'd discovered the truth about himself. Only lately, that dream had begun to change. He had a place of his own now and a family. A strange sort of family that actually included humans, but they *were* his family.

"Aren't you curious?" Trevor asked, his eyes guarded. "Don't you want to see it? Don't you want to be there when everything changes?"

Michael felt another surge of that old longing.

What would it be like to stand on the planet where his parents were born? Would the air feel more *right* in his lungs? Would everything feel somehow familiar?

"You don't have to give me an answer right now or anything," Trevor said, breaking the silence and looking out at the shore again. "Just know I want you there."

FIVE

Liz peered into the refrigerator. It was crammed with food—Crashdown stuff, some of her mama's baking experiments, a batch of her *abuelita*'s tamales—but nothing looked good to her. She reached over and pressed the long white button that controlled the little light inside the fridge, then released it. On. Off. On. Off.

"I remember when you figured out that mechanism," a voice said behind her. She turned around and saw her papa smiling at her. "You were about, oh, six, and you were determined to know whether the light stayed on when the door was closed. I think your sister was doing a unit in school about energy conservation, and that's what set you off."

"I don't even remember that," Liz told him. She pushed the fridge door closed, struck by how easily he had brought her sister, Rosa, into the conversation. That was a change. A change for the better.

"Want me to make you something?" he asked, leaning into the counter. "Remember, before I owned the Crashdown, I was the fastest short-order cook in the West." He ran his fingers over his bald spot. "Back when my hair managed to completely cover my scalp."

"No thanks. I'm not really hungry," Liz answered. She had a feeling she was supposed to laugh at her father's joke, but she wasn't up to it.

"Just saying good night to the food?" he asked.

Just avoiding going to bed, Liz thought. Every time she lay down under the blankets, waves of grief smashed into her until she could hardly breathe. It didn't take a rocket scientist to figure out why. When she was alone in bed, it brought up all kinds of memories of Adam. Their most special times together had been on the dream plane, and now whenever she began to drift off to sleep, entering that almost dreaming stage, Adam's face would appear before her, eyes bright and hopeful, so eager to try new things. Things he would never have the chance to experience now.

"Liz?"

She realized she hadn't answered her papa's question. "Um, yeah, saying good night. It's lonely in the fridge in the dark," she said quickly, forcing a fake laugh. She flashed on an image of Adam. Alone in the dark, deep under the desert floor.

"Is something wrong?" her papa asked. "I mean, besides the plight of the friendless vegetables?"

"No, I'm just sort of tired," Liz said, going into reassure-the-parent mode. She didn't want to upset her father. She didn't want to give him any reason to worry about her. She—

Stop, she ordered herself. He doesn't need your protection. Liz pulled in a deep breath and met her father's warm brown eyes. "Actually, something—something bad happened. Something awful," she admitted.

Her papa pulled a chair away from the kitchen table and gestured for her to sit. As soon as she did, he sat down beside her. "Whatever it is, you can tell me."

"I had this friend . . . Adam?" She looked at her dad to see if the name struck a memory, but it didn't seem to. "Well, you might have met him in the Crashdown once. He's . . . dead."

Her father shifted in his seat, and Liz told herself to slow down and choose her words carefully. She could tell her father what she was feeling, but she couldn't tell him everything.

"He—" She broke off. There were some things that still had to be kept secret, even from him. "He was . . . he was in a burger place in Hobbs, and he ordered a fish sandwich," Liz continued. "Then he left, and a drunk driver hit him. He's dead." Her voice wobbled as she realized for the hundredth time that he really *was* dead.

It wasn't even close to the truth. And it was a totally lame cover-up. But it still conveyed how random Adam's death had been.

Her father shook his head. "*Mija*, you're still a baby. You shouldn't have to know that the world can be so painful. I wish I could—"

"Protect me?" Liz interrupted.

"Yes!" her father burst out angrily. Liz noticed that his hands were curled into fists on top of his thighs.

"I know. I understand," Liz told him. "But you can't."

He let out a sigh that sounded like it came all the way up from his toes. "That's a hard thing you're asking me to accept," he admitted. "I'm your papa. Protecting you should be part of the job." He sighed again, his fists loosening. "But you're right. There are some things I can't control." He lifted one hand and placed it over hers on top of the table. "I can keep you company, though, right? And that helps a little, not having to go through something hard alone."

"It helps a lot," she answered, not trying to protect him or make him feel better. Just telling him the truth. Change for the better.

They sat for almost an hour, mostly in silence, sometimes chatting about customers at the Crashdown or something her papa had read in the newspaper. Liz felt something inside her unclench as they hung out together.

Finally he yawned. Then she yawned. Then he yawned again. Then she yawned again. "Copycat," her papa said.

Liz used the tabletop to push herself to her feet. She gave the lazy Susan a spin, watching the daisy in the center twirl. "I'm falling asleep sitting here. I'm going to bed," she announced.

"Anytime you want to talk about Adam or anything else, I'm sure the vegetables will be happy to listen," her papa teased. "Or if they've been made into a salad, you can come find me."

"Thanks," Liz answered. She kissed his bald spot, then headed out of the kitchen. Behind her she heard her father begin to hum one of his favorite Grateful Dead songs, a sure indicator that he was feeling good.

And so was she. Well, better, anyway. A little lighter somehow. Liz walked quietly into her bedroom, undressed, and climbed into bed as quickly as she could, trying to hold on to that lightness. She began to drift off to sleep almost immediately. Adam's face flickered briefly in the darkness behind her eyelids, but the image didn't cause quite as much pain as it usually did. It just means he's inside me, she thought sleepily, the way I told him he would be.

With a dizzying rush she crossed the border between sleep and wakefulness. She was dreaming, but she also knew she was dreaming. I wonder why I'm dreaming this? she thought. She was sitting in the bleachers of some kind of aquatic show. A blond girl, dressed in white, stepped into view and started a spiel about the very talented dolphin they were about to see. She asked for a volunteer from the audience and picked Liz, even though everyone around Liz had been waving their hands wildly and she hadn't even raised hers.

Obediently Liz stepped up next to the girl in white. The girl handed her a fish and told her to walk out onto the end of the diving board. Liz stared up at the high dive in question. "The dolphin isn't going to be able to jump that high, is it?" she asked. The steps leading up to the board went up for what seemed like five stories.

"It's a very special dolphin," the girl answered. "It's

not from around here." And suddenly, without climbing the steps, Liz was on the diving board. She carefully made her way out to the end and held the fish over the water, using just her thumb and forefinger.

She peered down at the turquoise pool below. "There's no way any dolphin can make it all the way up here," she muttered.

Almost as the words left her mouth, a dolphin nearly as blue as the water, an amazing, light, bright blue, flew straight up into the air as if powered by *power.* Liz stretched out her hand, and the dolphin's muzzle pressed against it.

At the touch of its warm skin, Liz's bones felt like they had turned to liquid. It was Max. She knew it. The dolphin was Max.

Before she could speak, the dolphin was hurling back toward the pool. "Jump again!" she shouted down. "Jump—"

The next word got jammed in her throat. There was something else in the pool now. Something much bigger than the dolphin. Black and white. A whale. A killer whale.

"Get it out of there," she screamed, scanning the ground for the woman in white. But she was gone. And the water was already turning red, red with blood. So much blood.

"Max!" Liz screamed.

She bolted straight up in bed, slick with sweat. "It was him," she whispered, shoving her hair off her forehead. "He came into my dream."

Was the whale some piece of the consciousness that had entered her dream, too, trying to keep Max from communicating with her?

Liz lay back down and closed her eyes tightly. "Try again, Max," she said. "I'll try, too."

Michael's awareness of the room around him sharpened. He felt one of the flattened beanbags on the living-room floor under his feet, and he heard the clock in the kitchen mooing out the time. And he was back. All the molecules in his body re-formed.

"My heart still hammers like crazy every time I teleport in this body," Trevor complained.

"It's called fear. You have to accept the fact that you're a wuss," Michael joked. "I have a human body, too, and my heart rate is totally normal."

"Well, aren't you special?" Trevor shot back.

"I am," Michael bragged. He looked his brother in the eye and grinned. "And that's why I think you're right. You're going to need me to help reform society or whatever."

"You're coming back with me?" Trevor exclaimed.

"If we shatter the consciousness, yeah," Michael answered. He'd been thinking about it nonstop ever since Trevor had asked him, and he kept coming to one conclusion. How could he not? His brother had asked for his help. And he couldn't go his entire life without ever seeing the place he came from.

Trevor actually jumped in excitement and slapped Michael on the back. "It's going to be so great. There's so much I want to show you, all these people I want you to meet, and—" He snapped his mouth shut and looked at the floor. "I'm gushing now."

"Like I said, you're a wuss," Michael answered, but a gigantic goofy grin was spreading across his face. His big brother was all excited about taking Michael places. Another cool moment. "Uh, I've got to go pick up the car. I'll be back in a while," he said, needing to get his goofy face somewhere else until it returned to normal again.

"Bring back some of those green alien-head sugar cookies from the grocery store, okay? And some pesto," Trevor said.

"Yes, dear," Michael answered. "But when we're in public, and people know that we're brothers, I'd rather you keep your pesto-eating habits to yourself. Pesto is for, well, wusses."

Trevor rolled his eyes, and Michael trotted down the circular staircase, dodging one of Trevor's shoes as he went, then hurried out of the museum. He checked his watch as he started down Main Street. After midnight. Good. Maria would probably be asleep.

He decided to walk over to her place instead of taking the bus. That way there'd be an even better chance she'd be making z's when he got there.

Not that he couldn't wake her up. He'd woken her up lots of times, crawling through her window in the early morning. But he had to break that little habit cold turkey. If he was going back to the home planet—no, make that *when* he went back to the home planet—he didn't want Maria to have to go through some kind of Michael withdrawal. He'd use the time until they shattered the consciousness to sort of break her of her Michael habit—wean her off him. And he was going to start by not hanging out in her bedroom late at night.

Michael turned onto Maria's street. He kept his eyes on the Caddy in the driveway, not letting himself check to see if the light in her window was on because on or off, he wasn't going in.

He took the car keys out of his pocket as he cut across the lawn and circled over to the driver's-side door. He pulled it open—and his breath left his lungs with a whoosh.

Maria was curled up on the front seat. Her raspberry-colored lips were partially open, and her sweater had slipped off one shoulder, revealing a stretch of creamy skin and a bright orange bra strap.

His fingers itched with the desire to run across that skin. His mouth tingled with the longing to kiss those lips until Maria woke up and wrapped her arms around him. Because that's what she would do. It had been a long time since Michael had kissed Maria, but he remembered exactly how it would feel, her tongue brushing against his, her hands pulling him even closer.

Do the words *wean her off* mean anything to you? Michael asked himself. How about *cold turkey*?

He closed the door as quietly as he could, then turned and ran back down the street.

Alex leaned against the locker next to Michael's, going for a casual, just-hanging-out-with-my-bud kind of feel. "I think my next list for the web site is going to be the top ten things a guy looks for in a girl. So, uh, what do you look for?"

He felt like a total dweeb, but Michael didn't seem to notice anything unusual. Which wasn't exactly a comforting thought.

You're doing this for Maria, Alex reminded himself. A little reconnaissance mission. He hadn't told her he was going to try to squeeze some info out of Michael. If he found out anything good—like that Michael went for girls who were into aromatherapy—he'd pass it on. If, on the other hand, Michael told him he was a Xena, Warrior Princess kind of guy, then, well, this conversation never happened.

"Skin," Michael answered.

"Skin?" Alex repeated. "Like showing a lot of skin?"

Michael pulled a bag of Hog Phasers, Roswell's answer to spicy pork rinds, out of his locker and held it out to Alex. Alex checked to make sure Michael hadn't added chocolate sauce or anything yet, then took a handful.

"Showing a lot would be okay, but what I really mean is, I like soft, smooth skin, you know?" Michael pulled out a can of whipped cream and sprayed some into the bag.

"I'm a butt man myself," Doug Highsinger offered from the end of the row of lockers. He grabbed a stack of books and slammed his locker closed.

"You certainly are," Alex joked. "I already did the top ten favorite body parts list. I'm looking for other . . . *qualities,* I guess you'd call them."

"Oh. Well, then, I have nothing more to add." Doug wandered off with a half salute.

"So you're looking for stuff like a good sense of humor." Michael crammed three of the Hog Phasers into his mouth and chewed loudly.

"Yeah. Exactly," Alex said, crossing his arms in front of his chest. "Is that something that's important to you—a good sense of humor?" Because that would be great, he thought. Maria didn't make hilarious jokes or anything. In fact, she usually made really lame ones. But she was always finding something to laugh at, and that was the best kind of sense of humor, if you asked him.

Michael licked a smear of whipped cream off his top lip and shook his head. "Hasn't it completely sunk in that pretty much any girl in school would go out with you if you looked at her cross-eyed?" he demanded. "You don't have to suck up with some sensitive-guy list on your web page. Those days are over, my friend."

"I wasn't—," Alex began to protest.

Michael slammed his locker shut. "Gotta go. I'm

meeting up with Trevor and Maria. Good luck to you and the B team." He strode off down the hall.

"You guys are the B team," Alex called after him, then shrugged and headed out to the parking lot. Liz and Isabel were already waiting for him in the Jeep. He swung himself into the back. "Hi ho, hi ho, it's off to work—" Alex stopped himself. "Sorry. Pulled another Maria. I can't get Snow White out of my head."

"Oh, just so you know," Liz said as Isabel pulled out of the parking lot. "Maria said if she ever heard you use that expression again, she was going to use your head for a planter. For an herb garden or something."

"The truth hurts—that's her problem," Alex answered, stretching out his arms and resting them on top of the backseat. "I brought some cards. I thought we could play poker if Max—" He stopped himself. "And yes, folks, your eyes didn't deceive you, that *was* his foot going into his mouth for a second time."

"Yeah. Watch it. Or the expression will quickly become pulling an Alex," Isabel warned, glancing at him in the rearview mirror as her blond hair whipped around her face.

Alex decided to keep his mouth shut the rest of the way to the UFO museum. Liz and Isabel didn't bother trying to make conversation, either. There was obviously some mental gearing up happening on both their parts as they prepared for the Max encounter.

It wasn't exactly a picnic for Alex to see Max in his comaesque state. But Max wasn't his brother. He wasn't the love of Alex's life. It just didn't rip him up inside in the same way it did Isabel and Liz. Both of them were walking wounded.

"Hi ho, hi ho," Isabel said sarcastically as she pulled into the museum parking lot.

"You want me to just run upstairs and check on him?" Alex asked, looking up toward Michael's apartment. "If he's still out, I could give him the speech about wanting to find the Stones for him—in case *anybody* in there's listening—then we could go to Flying Pepperoni for a while and do another check later."

"I want to see him," Isabel said, unlatching her seat belt. "Now."

"So do I," Liz insisted. They each gave him a semi-disgusted look, then climbed out of the Jeep.

"Okay, okay. Just a suggestion." The girls had guts. No taking the easy way for either of them, Alex thought as he followed them up the outside staircase leading to the apartment.

"The TV's on!" Isabel cried when she reached the front door. She jerked it open and ran into the living room. Max was sitting on the floor, eyes focused on the set.

"Hey, you're awake! Who kissed you?" Alex called as he burst into the room. His heart felt like it was on an elevator going up. Max was the center of their group, the backbone, the leader, the . . . Alex couldn't come up with another one. His brain was on overload. Max was the Max.

"Max!" Liz exclaimed. "What happened? Are you okay?"

He didn't turn his head. Alex's internal elevator was going straight down, no stops. Something was very wrong.

"Did you find the Stones?" Max asked, finally looking over at them. His blue eyes were alert. But there was something missing.

"It's not him," Liz said, her voice low and strained.

Alex gave a quick nod to let her know he got it. "Not yet," he told the consciousness. "We're planning to go out to the cave today."

"We talked it over, and we think there's a good chance Michael stashed them there," Isabel added, her voice sounding normal even though her entire body was rigid. "Not that he would tell us or anything."

"Let's go," the consciousness said through Max. Clearly it was accessing his knowledge of the language and of earth itself. Alex hoped it was careful as it went digging through Max's brain. Who knew what kind of damage it could do in there?

"The Jeep's right downstairs," Alex answered. All we have to do is keep the consciousness entertained, he reminded himself. When we don't find the Stones at the cave, we'll just drive it somewhere else—anywhere else.

"Good." The Max thing rose to its feet and headed for the door. Alex, Isabel, and Liz exchanged wary looks but silently followed.

"I'm driving," Isabel announced when they hit the parking lot. She trotted to the driver's side and scrambled behind the wheel before *Max* had a chance to respond. Alex nudged Liz toward the shotgun seat, then climbed in the back. If anyone was going to have to share a seat with a dangerous alien contingency, it was going to be him. The Max thing got in beside him.

"Hey, Max, we have Trevor taking your place at home," Isabel said as she drove through town, heading for the highway. "I think Mom and Dad like him a little more than they do you." She shot a fierce glance over her shoulder at Max's face. Alex didn't have to check to see if she'd shocked some kind of reaction out of the real Max. Isabel's devastated expression gave him the answer. She turned back to the road and sped up.

"Max, look! UFOnics!" Liz called out, her voice high and too loud. "Remember that time that I went there with Jerry Cifarelli and you were jealous and you changed your face and went in so you could spy on us?" She twisted around, gripping the roll bar in both hands. "Remember, Max?" Her voice broke on his name, but she kept going, taking her turn at trying to jar Max free. "And it didn't work because you forgot to change your eyes, and so I knew it was you. Remember?"

The anti-Max turned to Alex, ignoring Liz. "If the Stones aren't in the cave, where do we try next?"

Alex wished he could head butt Max for the pain he'd just caused Isabel and Liz. But he couldn't hurt the consciousness by hurting Max's body, not much, anyway.

"We could do a day trip to Carlsbad Caverns,"

Alex suggested. "Maybe even a weekend thing. It's huge, so searching it could take some time."

Alex struggled to remember some factoid about the caverns. "There's one room—that's what they call the different parts of the caverns—rooms—named the Hall of Giants," he volunteered. "It has some really tall rock formations in it . . . which is why it's named the Hall of Giants."

The Max thing twisted its lips in a condescending smile. Bring it on, Alex thought, ready to babble all night if that's what it took to keep the consciousness occupied. And make it leave Liz and Isabel alone.

"Let's see if I've got this right—while I was driving the car home yesterday, you two were frolicking in the ocean," Maria said. She slid off the hood of the Cadillac and glared from Michael to Trevor and back, trying not to let herself get distracted by the image of said wet-male frolicking.

"Not frolicking," Trevor told her, absentmindedly drawing in the desert sand with the toe of his work boot as he leaned against the car. "Like we said, we were able to test the power of the Stones by using them to heat up the water in the ocean. At first we just did a little section."

"So you could frolic," Maria shot back, noticing what Trevor had drawn in the sand was a big, curling wave.

"Then we realized that we could use the ocean as a way to fully test the combined power of the Stones," Trevor continued.

"The bad news is, forming a connection and using the Stones together didn't give us much more juice than each of us using the Stones separately," Michael added. He adjusted his weight on his leg so it wasn't pressing into the side of the hood ornament.

"Which means we're looking for another way to boost the Stones' power," Maria said.

"Yeah," Michael agreed.

"Yeah," Trevor repeated.

Silence descended. Too bad none of them had a clue how to do it.

Michael stretched out on the hood, staring up at the sky as if looking for inspiration. Maria tried not to look at the strip of naked stomach that Michael's scrunched-up shirt was now exposing. It gave her a certain kind of inspiration, but definitely not the kind she needed.

Stones. She needed to be thinking about the Stones. How could they be enhanced?

Maria forced her gaze away from Michael and over to Trevor. "I guess it wouldn't help for you two to connect with me? I mean, I can add a little bit of energy, but probably not enough."

"Probably not," Trevor answered, but he said it in a nice way. Maria was liking Michael's brother more and more as she got to know him. But as similar as he and Michael were, Trevor just didn't get to her the way Michael did. Looking at Trevor was enjoyable. Looking at Michael was almost meltdown inducing.

"Wait. Wait. That almost made me think of something." Michael sat up fast.

"What?" Trevor asked.

"*Almost* made?" Maria chimed in.

"Shut up," Michael snapped at them, running his fingers through his black hair until it was spikier than ever. "Just wait. I got this flash of a thing. An idea."

Trevor gave Maria the raised-eyebrow look. She gave it back, but she had to use her fingers to make her eyebrow go as high as his did.

"Okay, connecting with Maria is a stupid idea. It would hardly do anything," Michael burst out.

"That's been established, thank you very much," Maria muttered, blushing for no reason.

Michael ignored her and turned to Trevor. "But what if the two of us connected to Max? It might take the power of all three Stones to shatter the consciousness from the outside. But if we link to Max, we link to the consciousness, and then we'd be using the power of the two Stones from the *inside.*"

Maria's stomach dropped. Destroying something from inside Max didn't sound appealing to her.

"It could work," Trevor answered slowly. "The consciousness might be much more vulnerable from the inside. But there's no way of testing your theory. Max is the only being on earth connected to the consciousness."

"What's the downside of trying it?" Maria asked, hoping they might see how dangerous this could be. "I mean, do you have any idea if the consciousness could sense what was happening and . . . retaliate?"

Trevor shrugged helplessly. "I don't have any more information than you do. It's never been attempted."

"It wouldn't be the first time we've done things that have never been tried," Michael said. He tried to smooth down a few of his spikes, but it didn't work. "But who knows if the human body can even withstand having the power of the Stones directed into it?"

"Exactly," Maria said, remembering the way the Stone's power sliced straight through Adam's heart. Her mouth was suddenly very dry.

"When I used a Stone on DuPris, I didn't hold back," Trevor said. "I detonated it right into his body. I don't know if any entity could take that kind of blast without—"

"Going splat?" Maria finished for him. She wiped her hand across her face, as if flecks of DuPris's bone and blood were still spattered there.

"Once we're in, we might be able to direct the power at the consciousness without sending it full force through Max," Trevor said, lacing his hands together and putting them behind his head. "But I don't think we'd be able to avoid giving him some kind of jolt."

"Why not try it on me?" Maria swallowed hard. "That's what a lovely assistant is for, right? Just connect and give me a little, teeny bit of the Stones' power."

"No way," Michael said immediately.

Her heart jumped at the quickness of his protective response, but she wasn't about to back down. "Why not?" she demanded. "It's safer to test it on me. The consciousness won't be alerted, and if . . . if something goes wrong, you guys can heal me."

"If we just do a little, just to see the human

body's reaction to a low dose . . ." Trevor let his words trail off as Michael shook his head. "No way. We can't risk it."

"It's for Max. I want to do it for Max," Maria insisted. "And besides—" She looked Michael right in the eye and touched his arm. "I trust you not to let me get hurt. At least not permanently."

At least not permanently *physically,* she added to herself. Emotionally was a whole other story.

Michael stared at her for what seemed like an eternity, and a few times she thought he was about to say something, but he stopped himself. Maria's heart was beating a mile a minute.

"Okay, but we'll take it very slowly," Michael said finally. "If anything goes wrong, even the slightest bit, we break the connection."

"Agreed," Trevor answered. He pulled one of the Stones out of his pocket and put one hand on Maria's left arm. Michael stepped over, Stone already in his fist, and gently wrapped his fingers around her right arm.

I hope they don't get anything too embarrassing off me, Maria thought as they made the connection. The Stone in Trevor's free hand began to glow with a blue-green light. The Stone in Michael's glistened purple-green.

Maria closed her eyes, trying not to panic. Don't think of *splat,* she ordered herself. Don't think of *splat.* She repeated the words over and over until Michael interrupted her.

"How are you feeling?" he asked.

"Is it over? Did you do it? Am I bleeding?" Maria exclaimed, her eyes still squeezed tightly shut.

"You're not bleeding," Michael answered. "Do you feel like you should be bleeding? Does something hurt?"

"No. No. I was just wondering," Maria said. She thought she heard a snicker. "You better not be laughing at me!" she warned them, without opening her eyes. She'd open them when this was over, not one second before.

"We're just going to try a little more," Trevor told her. "And no one is laughing."

"Okay. Good." She began her mantra again. Don't think of *splat.* Don't think of *splat.*

"Yow!" she cried as she felt her feet leave the ground. Her eyes flew open despite herself. She was eye to eye with Michael. And she was . . . okay. "So this is what it's like to be tall," she said, glancing around. "I like."

"No pain?" Trevor asked.

Maria turned her head toward him, and her body followed. "I'm good," she told him.

"Let's go up just a degree," Michael said.

Maria slowly rose another two feet. She flapped her arms up and down. The guys got the message. A second later she was swooping and darting through the air. "I'm a ballerina bird," she exclaimed, starting off on one of her uncontrollable giggle fits.

"Is she hyperventilating?" she heard Trevor ask.

"No, she's just being Maria," Michael answered with a smirk.

"More! Do more!" Maria begged. And she was dropped into a rolling nosedive, then pulled out just before she reached the desert floor.

"Better than any amusement park ride, huh?" Michael shouted up to her.

Maria giggled even harder as the power twirled her through a triple somersault, then skimmed her low enough to touch Michael and Trevor's heads.

"We don't have anything like amusement parks on the home planet," Trevor said. "When we go back, we should open one. We could call it Guerin brothers. The Guerin makes it kind of exotic sounding."

Maria stopped giggling so abruptly that she bit her tongue. The taste of blood filled her mouth. She couldn't have possibly heard what she thought she'd just heard. Michael was planning to go back home with Trevor? And he didn't think this was important enough to even tell her?

"Let me down!" she yelled. "I think I'm going to be sick." The second her feet touched the ground, Maria bent over, wrapping her arms around her stomach.

I don't mean anything to him, she thought. He can just leave. Maybe kiss me good-bye. Maybe not. Just see ya. Adios. I'm outta here.

A moment later she felt Michael's hand rubbing her back. "Was it too much power, you think?"

She jerked her body away. "No. I'm fine. I just got dizzy."

"There's not much point in doing more experiments with Maria," Trevor said, pocketing his Stone.

"It can only tell us so much about what will happen with Max."

"We'll just have to go for it. Tomorrow the two of us will connect and see what happens," Michael answered.

"No!" Maria snapped upright. She was in full panic mode on so many levels, she had no idea why she was thinking clearly, but she was. Maybe panic was the key to a clearer mind. "I just realized that now that the consciousness is aware of what's going on, Trevor can't go near Max."

Michael blinked, and Maria knew he was impressed she'd thought of something that hadn't occurred to him. Not that it mattered to him, really.

"She's right," Michael said. "It would go ballistic if it saw you. It knows you're one of the rebels who want to destroy it."

"So now what?" Maria asked. She struggled to keep all her attention focused on the Max crisis. If she let herself think about Michael anymore, she'd lie down right here and never, ever get up.

"So I make the connection to Max and use both of the Stones myself," Michael answered.

"I don't know if that's such a good idea," Maria said.

"I'm doing it," he said in that firm Michael way that left no room for questions.

And that was that. There was nothing Maria could do once Michael had made up his mind.

SEVEN

"I drove your car to school today—again, since you didn't pick it up—again," Maria told Michael as she came up behind him in the hall after the last bell. "It's in the lot."

He nodded. She'd already told him that at lunch.

"My mom's threatening to make you pay some kind of driveway rental fee," Maria continued, pulling her curls back from her face and letting them bounce right back again.

"Sorry," he muttered as they headed out to the parking lot to meet up with the others. He'd kept putting off going to Maria's last night, afraid he'd find her sleeping in his car again, and he just didn't feel like he could deal with that. Not kissing her had been hard enough the first time.

Man, why had that moron Alex asked him what he wanted in a girl? The question had gotten stuck in his head somehow, and every time he thought of an answer, it had something to do with Maria. Now he couldn't stop thinking about the girl, which wasn't exactly making Operation Cold Turkey easy to carry out.

About halfway across the lot Maria grabbed the back of Michael's shirt with both hands and pulled him to a stop. He turned to face her, and their bodies brushed together, sending a shiver straight through him. He could smell eucalyptus oil on her and the cedar oil she always used when she was stressed. Mixed with that, something sweet and flowery. Michael took a step back. "What?" he said, his voice coming out harsh and hoarse.

"I know you never listen to me. I know I have no influence over you. But Michael, I really don't think you should try to shatter the consciousness alone," Maria said in a rush, her blue eyes wide. "What about Isabel? Couldn't she—"

Michael took another step away from her. Her scent was fogging his brain. "Isabel hasn't had any practice with the Stones," he answered.

Maria closed the distance between them until their bodies were almost touching again. "So take a couple of days and let her practice," she begged in a whisper.

"I can handle it," Michael told her. He turned and started toward the Cadillac again, Maria trotting to keep up with his long strides. "And if it's dangerous, it's better that only one of us is at risk."

He heard a horn honk and glanced over. The Jeep was pulling out of the lot with Isabel, Liz, Trevor, and Alex inside. Which left Michael and Maria making the trip to the UFO museum in the Caddy—alone. Great. Yeah, this was great. He needed to be concentrating, focusing, getting ready to shatter the freaking consciousness.

Now all these Maria thoughts would keep invading

his head. Not to mention all the Maria smells. And the closeness of the Maria skin. Michael climbed into the car and slammed the door as hard as he could.

The second Maria got in beside him, he threw the gearshift into reverse and jerked the car out of its parking space. He saw Maggie McMahon getting ready to pull out, but he cut her off. There was no time to be nice and polite. The sooner he got out of this car and away from Maria, the better off they'd both be. It was only fair to Maria to taper off his contact with her. And as for touching of any kind—even basic friend touching—there would be no more of that. He really had to go cold turkey. Maybe it would help if he imagined her skin was . . . cold turkey. Instead of soft. Instead of warm. He glanced at her bare shoulder peeking out from her tank top. Instead of very, very tempting.

"You nervous?" Maria asked, fidgeting with her colorful beaded bracelets.

"No. Of course not," he snapped.

"Oh." She reached over and ran one finger lightly across the back of his hand, and he almost veered into oncoming traffic. "So the way your knuckles have turned all white, that's just normal?"

Michael realized he was gripping the wheel way, way too tightly. He forced his fingers to relax, letting the blood flow return to them.

"Don't touch me while I'm driving, okay?" he said. He checked the rearview mirror. He checked the side mirror. He checked the street in front of him. There was a little splotch on the windshield, and Michael hit the button to squirt some water on it, then started the wipers. Lots of stuff to think about when operating a vehicle, he thought. Lots of non-Maria stuff. He snapped the wipers off and scanned the gauges—no attention available to think about Maria. Or the way her lips really were almost the color of raspberries. Juicy raspberries. Sweet raspberries.

"Michael, we just passed the museum," Maria announced, glancing behind them, confused.

Crap. Michael made a squealing U-turn, eliciting a little squeal from Maria, and pulled into the museum parking lot. He got out of the car in record-breaking time without a second glance at his passenger.

The rest of their friends were waiting outside, and Trevor walked over to Michael as he hurried toward the outdoor stairs that led to his apartment.

"I'll wait down here," Trevor said. "Come get me as soon as it's over. Or have someone else call me if . . ."

He didn't finish the thought, but Michael knew what he was about to say—if you're getting beaten so badly, you need backup just to get out alive.

"I will," Michael promised solemnly. It seemed like there should be something else to say, but he couldn't think what it was.

"You two could hug, you know," Maria said from behind him. "You *are* brothers and everything."

Michael and Trevor stared at each other. Then, with a what-the-hell shrug, Michael jerked his brother to him and hugged him tightly, releasing him with a thump on the back. Very manly.

"We'd better get up there," Michael said. He reached into his pocket and wrapped his fingers around the Stones, then trotted up to the stairs and took them two at a time. Isabel, Liz, Alex, and Maria were right behind him, causing the steps to creak and moan as the crew pounded upward. Michael was comforted to know they were there, but he was ready to get this thing *done*.

"Is there any way we can help once we get inside?" Alex asked, just behind Michael. It was better than having Maria right there, Michael supposed.

"Nope," he answered firmly, sounding calm. He yanked open the door and strode into the living room, where he could hear the TV on. He found the Max thing sitting in front of the tube, which was where it had been when he left for school that morning. Michael walked straight over to him—it. "Hey, Max. I've been thinking about it a lot, and Isabel and Liz and Alex are right. If you want to get home, we should all be helping you."

Here goes, he thought. He clamped his hand down on Max's shoulder and focused on making the connection.

Am I in? Michael thought. He wasn't getting any images, the way he usually did when he connected, but he had felt kind of a *click*—a meeting of two pieces.

He pulled in a deep breath and let it out slowly, trying to relax, trying to let the images in. All he saw was blackness. Did the consciousness sense his intention? Was it trying to keep him out?

Max! Michael thought. Max! I'm here. But I'm getting blocked.

A rushing sound filled his ears, and he could feel pressure building inside his brain. Pushing from all sides. Squeezing his gray matter into a tennis-ball-size lump.

Michael's eyes began to water, feeling like they would pop any second with the pressure. The pressure . . .

He dug his fingers into Max's skin, refusing to break the connection. He knew the Stones could help him, but it was too soon to use them. He had to wait until he was sure he could direct the power into the consciousness.

The rushing sound grew louder. Something warm and wet trickled out of his left ear. Michael gathered all his energy and threw out one more mental shout. *Maaaax!*

The image of Max's face flared in Michael's mind, obliterating the darkness. He felt his brain expand, the horrible crushing pressure easing up, the roaring in his ears dimming. His whole body lightened until he was no longer sure if his feet were on the floor. Max's face disintegrated into a swirl of colors. The most beautiful colors Michael had ever seen. So rich and vivid, he could almost *feel* them.

He rolled onto a patch of tangerine, letting it soak into every pore, mix with his blood, seep through every cell membrane, stain his protons and electrons and neutrons. He became the color. And the color became him. And the tangerine Michael felt good.

Above him was an expanse of saffron yellow. He stretched out his arms and pulled the color toward him, opening his mouth so he could swallow it. It traveled like liquid fire down his throat and into his stomach. The heat turned Michael saffron from the inside out. And the saffron Michael felt good, too.

He spun, weightless, free, and spotted a geyser of indigo. He had to experience it. With a hoot of pleasure he propelled himself under the spray, tilting back his head, letting the color drench him, letting it—

"Michael! *No!*"

Michael snapped his head up. That was Max's voice.

You've got to get out! Now! Max ordered, speaking thought to thought with Michael.

Why? Michael thought back. He stared down at his indigo hands. They were so beautiful. His body was almost coated. But he wanted more. Needed it. He dove straight into the geyser.

Noooo!

Max's wail grew fainter, then cut off abruptly.

"Why is Michael smiling like that?" Maria whispered in Liz's ear, her face all scrunched up. "It's kind of . . . creepy."

Liz tore her eyes away from Michael and shot a quick glance at Maria. A little shiver ran from her shoulders to the base of her spine. "I don't know, but you're right."

Alex moved up closer behind them. Liz could feel his breath on the top of her head. "How do we think this is going?" he asked softly.

Liz forced herself to look down at Max's face. It was lifeless, just like always. Her blood was starting to pump faster, and she was getting tense. There were too many questions here. Too many unknowns. Who knew what was going on inside Max and Michael's heads?

"I have no idea," she said. She felt so helpless just standing here. Watching. Not even knowing exactly what she was watching *for.*

"If Michael had started using the Stones, we'd definitely see the glow, even through his pocket," Isabel said. She shifted a little closer to Liz, and now they were all standing in a tense little clump. "It seems like it's taking too long."

"Except this has never been done before, so there's really no way to know how long is too long," Alex offered.

"It just feels too long, okay?" Isabel snapped.

"I really don't like the way Michael's smiling," Maria said. None of them looked at one another when they were talking. The Max-Michael connection was just too riveting.

Liz didn't have any comforting response to Maria's comment, so she reached out and took Maria's hand. A moment later she felt Isabel grab her other hand. Alex stretched out his arms and managed to encompass all three of them.

And they watched. And waited. Each second stretching out until it felt as long as an hour.

Liz's eyes began to burn with the strain. She'd been trying not to blink too much just in case. You're not going to miss anything in two seconds, she told herself, letting her eyes close briefly.

A gasp escaped from deep in her throat when she opened them again. Max's face was twisted in agony. Then almost instantly it lost all animation, jaw slack, eyes dull.

"Did you see—," she began.

"Yes," Isabel answered, squeezing Liz's hand so hard, an arrow of pain zinged up her arm.

"What did it look like to you?" Liz demanded, keeping her eyes locked on Max in case there was another lightning change.

"What are you talking about?" Maria jumped in.

"Max's face—for a second it looked like he was himself again. And that something hideous was happening to him," Isabel answered. There were tears in her voice.

"I missed it," Alex said. He hadn't let go of them, and he squeezed a little tighter.

"I was looking at Michael," Maria admitted sheepishly.

Liz broke free from their little knot and slowly crossed the room toward Max and Michael. She circled them, looking for anything that might tell her what had happened, but they looked just like they had before. Maria, Alex, and Isabel joined her a moment later.

"Michael's hand," Maria choked out.

Liz's throat tightened as she lowered her gaze to Max's shoulder. She was definitely going to throw up.

"Tell me I'm wrong," Maria begged, her blue eyes wide with terror.

Liz reached out and gently gave Michael's wrist a tug. It didn't move. "You're not wrong," she told Maria. She swallowed hard before saying the next, completely ridiculous, but true words. "Michael's hand . . . it's started growing into Max's shoulder."

Isabel bolted toward the front door. "Trevor, get up here!" Liz heard her scream. Footsteps pounded up the stairs, then Isabel and Trevor burst back into the room. Trevor skidded to a stop in front of Michael and Max.

"Have you ever seen anything like this?" Alex barked. He was paler than Liz had ever seen him, and she knew she looked the same way. It was all she could do to keep from fainting at this point.

Trevor opened his mouth, then closed it and swallowed, as if his throat was suddenly too dry to let him speak. "No," he croaked out. "But it looks like—I think Michael is being absorbed into Max. Into the consciousness."

"Can we cut him free?" Liz asked, wincing at the thought of a knife penetrating Max's skin. "Only one of Michael's fingers is completely submerged, and it isn't deep. I can see the lump." She had to take a deep breath to keep from dry heaving.

There was a soft sucking sound, and as Liz watched, Michael's hand slid into Max's shoulder all the way up to the wrist.

"It's speeding up," Trevor said, sounding desperate.

"We've got to get him out!" Maria cried. She grabbed Michael by the shoulders and gave him a frantic shake. The Michael-Max thing swayed a little, but there was no other reaction.

Isabel turned to Trevor, her eyes wild. "What if we all form a connection, then connect to them?" she demanded. "Could we pull them apart that way?"

"I don't know any more than you do," he said, pushing his hands through his hair. "It might work. Or we might be abs—"

"Let's try it," Maria interrupted. She grabbed Liz's hand, then Alex's. Liz's heart thumped with fear, but she squeezed Maria's freezing cold fingers, moved closer to Max, and took his limp hand, holding on tight enough for both of them.

A connection ignited between them as soon as the circle of hands was closed. Each of their auras was like a flame in a bonfire of color—her amber, Maria's sparkling blue, Alex's screaming orange, Isabel's deep purple, and Trevor's magenta.

Where was the jade green? Where was the brick red? Where was Max? Where was Michael?

As if in answer to her thought, a plume of liquid jade arched into the bonfire, followed by a curl of red. And the fire turned into a fountain, all their auras turning to arcs of fluid color that leaped over and under one another in a dance of joy.

Other streams of color joined the fountain—tangerine, indigo, saffron, fuchsia, lilac. The colors of the connection between Liz, Maria, Alex, Isabel, Trevor, Michael, and Max grew diluted. More new colors poured into the mix, each color losing its individuality until the fountain was mud brown.

Wrong. This is wrong, Liz thought. She shook her head and felt her curly hair fly around her face.

Curly hair? Liz didn't have curly hair. *Maria* was the one with the curly hair. All Liz could see was brown, brown everywhere. But she knew what was happening. They were becoming absorbed, melding together.

She tried to visualize the amber of her own aura. At first all she could come up with was the mud brown. But that wasn't right. Amber was lighter. Amber was like a perfect piece of Adam's toast. Like the scotch her papa sometimes drank. Like the honey Maria used instead of sugar. Like a lion's mane. Like the wood of her *abuelita*'s dresser.

A spray of pure amber erupted out of the mud. Yes!

Liz felt strong now. Strong and in control. She sent out an image to Maria—the blue of a sparkling blue lake, of the spangled tutus they'd worn in their ballet recital when they were little girls, of Maria's own blue eyes. And Maria's blue aura arced up beside Liz's amber one.

Alex must have figured out what he needed to do on his own because a geyser of orange burst free. Followed by one of purple and one of magenta.

Maria flung out an image of a Valentine's Day lollipop, the deep rich red of Michael's aura. Liz added the image of a stop sign. Alex threw in a mustang convertible with a red paint job so glossy, it looked edible. Isabel conjured up a hand with wicked-looking deep red nails. And Trevor added an image of Mars.

Liz scanned the expanse of mud. She didn't see anything red. But a small patch was bubbling. The bubbles grew bigger, started popping faster, then a vertical stream of red rose up.

Only one to go. Max! It's your turn, she thought. She concentrated fiercely on the image of a perfect emerald. Then she hurled it out as hard as she could.

And the connection broke.

Liz swayed on her feet as the living room of Michael's apartment reappeared around her. She twisted around so she could see Max's face, hoping, praying. But it was dull. Empty. No Max in there that she could see.

"Are you all right, Michael?" Isabel asked urgently.

Liz whirled around, her eyes going immediately to the hand that had been in Max's shoulder. It was free and appeared whole and fully functioning.

"I'm fine," Michael answered, flexing the fingers of the hand that had been absorbed. "But I guess it's time to move on to our fallback plan."

Silence fell over the group as they all looked at Max's lifeless body.

"The fallback plan we don't have," Alex reminded them all.

EIGHT

"Do I need to be Max now? Will your parents be home soon?" Trevor asked as he sat down on Isabel's soft, perfectly made bed.

"No. You have a couple of hours." Isabel picked up a glass kitten from her bedside table, then grabbed a Kleenex and started to polish the kitten furiously. "I keep thinking the consciousness is going to *do* something to Max. You know, to punish him for us trying to use the Stones against it."

Trevor opened his mouth to respond, but Isabel didn't give him a chance. She rushed on, scrubbing the kitten as hard as she could. "And then when we find a way to shatter the consciousness—*if* we do—then what will happen to him? You said you think Max could die. And that's not acceptable. That's—"

The glass kitten's tail snapped off in Isabel's fingers. She stared down at it, tears springing to her eyes. She wiped them away viciously, using both hands.

Trevor didn't bother trying to comfort her. He pretended not to even notice the tears since it was clear Isabel found them infuriating. Instead he took the kitten and the tail out of her hands, matched the pieces together, and used his power to nudge the molecules closer together, mending it. He set it back on the little table.

"I think the kitty's safer over here," he commented, forcing a smile.

Isabel gave a snort that blew a tiny, clear bubble out of one of her nostrils. He pretended not to notice that, either—although in a weird way, he found it kind of adorable.

He'd observed that when he was around Isabel, the heart of his human body beat a little faster, and sometimes a thin layer of sweat appeared between his fingers. He knew from studying the Kindred's materials that this was an expression of attraction. Humans were such a strange species. When he'd learned about the sensations, they sounded mildly repulsive, and the sweat sort of was. But the accelerated heartbeat was actually pleasurable, making his body feel warmer and somehow more alive.

He'd also observed that while Liz and Maria were as desirable in their own ways as Isabel, his human body didn't respond to them in the same way. Strange. Mysterious. He liked it.

"Thanks," Isabel muttered finally. "When I think about Max, I go a little crazy." She folded the Kleenex in half, then in half again.

A rush of guilt swept through Trevor, and he felt the back of his neck get hot. He'd been off on a little head vacation, thinking out the pleasures of attraction, while Isabel was clearly suffering.

If Isabel was a member of the Kindred, right

now she'd be sternly reminded that sacrifice was an honor. If Max died in the struggle to shatter the consciousness, it would be the most noble death he could have. But Trevor had no desire to lecture her.

"I wish I could give you all the answers," he said. "But I don't have any of them."

"I know," Isabel answered. She folded the Kleenex again, then again, then again until the little square couldn't get any smaller.

Trevor took it away from her. She frowned at him, but she didn't try to snatch it back. "I think we should go out somewhere," he said, struggling to come up with some way to make her feel even the tiniest bit better. "Tomorrow Michael and Maria and I are going to start working on the backup plan while you and Alex and Liz watch Max. So tonight let's just take a break."

"Take a break while Max could be getting tortured?" Isabel spat out, her face so red, it could have been on fire.

"Or I could go out and buy you a couple dozen more boxes of Kleenex so you can fold until you exhaust yourself," Trevor offered calmly.

Isabel combed her fingers through her hair and sighed. "I guess I wouldn't mind doing something that would make me totally exhausted so I could just fall into bed and sleep and wake up when there was actually something I could do for Max."

"Any ideas of what you want to do?" Trevor asked.

She tilted her head to one side, considering. "Dancing. UFOnics," she decided.

A half an hour later they were on the crowded dance floor. Every time he started thinking about what would happen if they couldn't come up with a backup plan, he danced harder. Every time he thought how devastating it would be to Isabel and the others if anything happened to Max, he danced harder. That was the advice he'd given Isabel when they'd first walked in. Don't think, just dance.

She seemed to be following it. Isabel danced with her eyes closed—clearly expecting everyone else to make sure they didn't run into *her*—blond hair flying as she spun this way and that.

Trevor's heart pounded as he watched her move, beating in his ears louder than the pulsating music. He felt the addition of a new chemical in his bloodstream, something that made him feel almost euphoric. He wondered if he'd ever respond to anyone this way back at home. Not with the furiously beating heart or the same chemicals of the human body, of course, but with this level of intensity.

He had no way to tell. Males and females were kept separate in the Kindred until it was time for them to start a birthing cycle. The Kindred believed that beings were more productive this way, and now Trevor could see why. If he felt like this at home, he'd never accomplish anything. All he'd want to do was follow around whoever gave him these sensations.

The music screamed to a halt, then started up

again, softer, slower. Isabel opened her eyes, her gaze going unhesitatingly to Trevor's. The skin between his fingers started pumping out the sweat.

"You still think my human form is, uh, yummy enough that any girl would want to dance with me?" he asked her, remembering the conversation they'd had at the UFO museum party.

"Definitely," she answered. UFOnics' colored lights made it difficult to see her aura, but Trevor thought the dancing had helped a little.

"Including you?" Trevor kept his gaze locked on hers.

Isabel answered by using the waistband of his pants to pull him toward her, then slipping her arms around his neck. He slid his hands around her waist, and they swayed back and forth, barely moving, hardly dancing.

But being this close to Isabel was all the distraction he needed. Right now every thought was of her, every nerve in his being responding to her. When she pressed her cheek against his shoulder, sliding her body even closer, he could feel her heart beating, beating fast.

The realization that Isabel could be feeling the same way about him that he was feeling about her—at least right this second, in this moment away from the rest of the universe, away from time, away from thought—left him almost breathless.

Liz sat under an enormous weeping willow tree, its long, drooping branches creating a private room for her. A room of green. A tiny tea set was arranged in front of her, the itty-bitty roses on the cups and saucers drawn with amazing detail. She took a sip from the nearest cup and tasted a drop of honey on her tongue. There was one other cup on the other side of the little teapot. But who was it for? She was all alone here.

She peeked past the green curtain-wall. Empty desert stretched out as far as she could see. Nobody out there anywhere.

"Would you like another cup, Liz, dear?" she asked herself. "Why, yes, I would. Thank you very much," she answered, smoothing the skirt of her cupcake dress. She picked up the pot and poured. Three raisins fell through the spout.

Liz wrinkled her brow. Raisins didn't belong in a teapot. And the dress with the cupcakes on it was from when she was in kindergarten. There's no way it would fit her now, but it did. And—and wait, something else was wrong—willow trees didn't belong in the desert.

I'm dreaming, Liz realized. Another one of those dreams where I know I'm dreaming.

Was Max in this dream, too? She scrambled to her feet and used both hands to part the branches of the willow tree wide. She scanned the desert. Was anything out there that could be Max in disguise?

All she saw was earth and sky. She seemed to be the only living creature. The willow tree was the only vegetation.

Liz returned to her place in front of the tea set, leaning back on the tree trunk. It felt soft and smooth beneath her head. Maybe I can call Max to me, she thought. It couldn't hurt to try, anyway.

She stared up at the canopy of jade green leaves over her head. "Max," she whispered. "Can you feel me here? Can you come to me? Please try." A branch of the willow tree brushed against her face. She flicked it away.

"I have two teacups and everything," she added. The branch brushed her cheek again, its leaves warm as flesh against her skin. Liz was struck by the memory of Max's fingers running down her face in exactly the same way.

"It's you!" she cried. "Willow trees don't have leaves this dark. Jade green—that's the color of your aura. It's you, Max!" The branch gently slid over her hair. Max loved to touch Liz's hair. It really was him.

"Okay, communication. That's what we need first," Liz muttered. She tried to send a loud, clear thought message to Max. Are you all right? Is there anything you can tell us about the consciousness that will help us get you free?

She strained for any murmur of a reply in her mind, but none came. "So no tree-to-human telepathy in this dream," she said.

But it *was* a dream. Yeah, she didn't have the powers that Max and the others did. But inside her own dream, couldn't she sort of create her own reality? Especially since she was aware that she was dreaming and everything?

"Maybe I could get some tree-to-tree telepathy

going." Liz concentrated on her feet, willing them to lengthen into roots that stretched into the ground.

The earth lurched beneath her. "It's working!" she cried.

Then with a groaning, crunching sound, the ground cracked open. Liz stumbled backward, barely managing to escape falling into the ravine that had formed—and swallowed the willow tree.

"No!" Liz shouted, staring down at the tree. Before she could take a step, the earth rumbled again, and the ravine began to close itself. In seconds the desert floor was smooth and flat again. As if the tree had never existed.

As if Max had never been there.

"Knock, knock," Maria's mother called, opening the bedroom door without waiting for an answer—one of her many annoying habits.

Maria hit the pause button on the remote and looked over at her mom. She was wearing Maria's black sweater that had shrunk in the wash. That sweater seemed to have moved permanently into her mom's closet. Majorly annoying.

"I might be a little later than usual tonight," Maria's mother announced. She shifted her weight slightly from foot to foot.

"Okay," Maria answered. She glanced at the still frame of the movie frozen on the TV screen—Karen Allen in midfaint. But did her mother take the hint that Maria wanted to get back to watching it? No.

"I'm going out with Daniel again," her mother said.

Maria sat up. "This is what? Like five times?" she asked, giving her mom her full attention.

"Uh-huh. I thought that—I'd heard that—the third date was significant, but . . ."

Don't go there, oh, please don't go there, Maria silently begged. She couldn't deal with talking about her mother's sex life.

"Or maybe that's just something I read in a magazine," her mom added quickly, seeming to realize that mentioning her surprise at not getting any on date three was way, way inappropriate.

"Maybe," Maria answered, her voice coming out like some weird kind of donkey bray.

"You know that perfume you mixed for me? I've been wearing it a lot lately—Daniel really likes it. And I just realized I ran out, and I really wanted to wear it tonight." Maria's mom looked at her hopefully. "He's picking me up in a few minutes."

"There isn't enough time to make a new batch," Maria answered. There really wasn't time, and even if there was, Maria wasn't sure how she felt about helping her mom snag a guy. She'd given up any fantasy of her parents getting back together, but still.

"Oh, okay. Never mind." Maria's mom nervously touched her hair, which Maria noticed was styled in a slightly different way. Tonight's really important to her, she realized.

"Wait," Maria said as her mother turned to leave. "I can get you something close. Sit," she instructed, patting the spot on the bed next to her. Her mother sat with a relieved smile.

Maria plucked two vials of essential oil off her bedside table. She took one of her mother's hands and flipped it palm up, then placed a few drops from each vial on her wrist and rubbed them in. A subcutaneous tremor ran through her mother's arm. Mom's nervous, Maria noticed. She rubbed a little harder, hoping to ease the tension from the muscles, but the quiver kept right on quivering.

"Thanks," Maria's mom said as Maria started working on the other wrist. "I just want to be . . . perfect." She touched her hair again self-consciously, then gave her midriff—bared by Maria's sweater—a hard poke. "Not that that's even possible."

I know the symptoms, Maria thought. Not only does Mom really, really like this guy, she's not sure how he feels about her. And she's worried that there is some significance, some he-doesn't-really-really-like-me-back significance, to five dates with no—

Maria stopped herself. She extremely did not want to go there.

"I think you look beautiful," she told her mother. "And you smell good, too."

The doorbell rang, and her mother lurched to her feet. "That's him!" She bolted toward the bedroom door.

"Mom!" Maria called, and her mother spun around to face her. "If he doesn't, um . . ." She decided to start over. "If he doesn't *appreciate* you, it's his loss."

"Aw, that's so sweet." Maria's mom rushed back

over and gave her a fast, lilac-and-vanilla-infused hug, then bolted out of the room.

Maria flopped back down into the nest of pillows on her bed.

"Okay, self, you take that advice, too," she muttered. "It's Michael's loss." She clicked the pause button again, and the movie started back up. A minute later she was entranced.

She was so completely immersed in the world of the movie that she practically flew off the bed when she heard her window slide open nearly an hour later.

"You scared me," she snapped, her heart pounding as Michael climbed into her room.

"It's not like it's the first time I've come in this way," he answered.

"Not lately." It came out sounding a lot more accusatory than she'd intended it to. Well, so what? It was the truth, wasn't it?

"What're you watching?" Michael asked. He took a step toward the bed, then veered off, grabbed the chair next to her dresser, and plopped down on it.

"Um, nothing. Nothing! I wasn't really watching anything. It was just background noise." Oh, God, where was the remote? What had she done with the remote? She scanned the bed, the bedside table, groped under the pillows.

"Looking for this?" Michael picked the remote off the floor but, being Michael, didn't hand it to her.

Maria lunged for the TV set, fumbling for the power button. She had to turn it off.

"Starman," Michael said. Too late. Maria glanced over her shoulder and saw him holding the plastic video rental box. "So you go out and rent stuff for background noise?" he asked, raising one eyebrow.

"Yeah, sometimes. Stupid, huh? That's me. Stupid," Maria babbled. She found the power button, hit it, and returned to the bed, sitting cross-legged and looking everywhere but at Michael.

He used the remote to click the TV back on. "Let's watch the rest. I've never seen it."

It will just be worse if I shut it off again, Maria thought. Not that it's not already totally obvious that I didn't want him to see what I was watching, which of course is why he now has to see it.

Michael stretched his legs out in front of him. Maria ordered herself not to check out the nice fit of his jeans. Of course, she didn't obey herself. "So what's happened so far?" he asked.

Ah, yes. Let's go for the maximum humiliation possible here, Maria thought.

"Well, that guy—" She nodded toward Jeff Bridges, who was in the middle of bringing a dead deer back to life. "He's the starman. His spaceship crash-landed, and he took on the form of Karen Allen's husband by using DNA from hair from a photo album. You know how some people save locks of hair?"

Maybe if Maria swamped Michael with details, he'd miss the fact that he'd caught her mooning over a movie that was a love story between an alien guy and a human girl.

"Anyway, he has to get back to his mother ship or he'll die, and some government people are chasing them, and a guy from SETI, too, who is basically decent. The starman, he really likes apple pie, and he just learned to drive. At first he thought a yellow light meant go very fast because he learned by watching Karen—I mean Jenny, the character's name is Jenny, Karen's the actress—drive and—"

"I'm up to speed," Michael said, cutting her off.

"Good," Maria answered. She scooted back a little farther so she could lean against the headboard and focused her eyes on the TV screen. She'd thought she'd have to pretend that she was having no problem watching it with him, but the story sucked her back in, and she didn't have to fake it after all.

When the movie got to the part where Jenny and Starman had to say good-bye, Maria's eyes got all wet and stingy, and she suddenly became aware that Michael was watching her and not the television.

Maria tried to stop the tears before they began rolling down her face, but she couldn't. Jenny's pain at never seeing Starman again was so real to her.

"Repeat after me. Movie. Reality. Movie. Reality," Michael said sarcastically.

She nodded and locked her teeth together, but she couldn't stop a muffled keening sound from escaping her. It was so sad.

Michael threw a box of Kleenex in her direction. "I've got to go," he told her.

Big surprise.

Maria wiped off her face and blew her nose hard.

"Wait," she commanded. She used another Kleenex on her face, sure it was already all blotchy. It was so unfair that she couldn't cry like Karen Allen, who looked beautiful and pale and tragic as her tears flowed.

"What?" Michael asked impatiently, getting to his feet and jamming his hands in his back pockets.

"Yesterday it sounded like Trevor expected you to go back home with him. So are you?"

She hadn't planned to ask Michael that question, even though she was dying to know the answer. But when he said he was leaving, it just came spilling out.

"Are you?" she repeated when he hesitated.

"I'm thinking about it," Michael answered.

And he was out of there, leaving Maria heartbroken and speechless.

NINE

Maria was already sitting at their usual booth at the back of Flying Pepperoni. Michael hesitated, trying to figure out if he should sit next to her or across from her. Next to her there could be some accidental skin-to-skin contact, and he'd definitely pick up the scent of the essential oils she wore. But across from her he'd have to look at her, and—

"Why are we stopping?" Trevor asked from behind him.

"We're not," Michael answered. He strode over to the table and slid onto the leatherette bench across from Maria, figuring it was marginally safer.

He still couldn't believe he'd gone to her house last night after all his mental lectures on the virtues of Operation Cold Turkey. At least he hadn't let himself sit on the bed, managing to utilize that much brain matter. And he hadn't touched her, even though when he'd seen the tears on her cheeks, he'd had this wild impulse to kiss them away and then just kiss her until the kiss became her whole world. And his.

What was wrong with him?

"Now that your entire party is here, would you

like to order?" Lucinda Baker asked as she bounced up to their booth.

"I wouldn't exactly call it a party," Maria muttered. She grabbed a bread stick out of the basket and broke it in half with a sharp snap.

"How about a batch of our buffalo chicken wings with our special blue cheese dipping sauce to get you started?" Lucinda continued cheerily.

"Lucinda, check the lost and found. I think I saw your pod in there," Maria said, crunching into the bread stick.

Lucinda lowered her voice. "The district manager is here today. And I'm supposed to be a—" She pointed to her big, yellow, I'm-a-happy-waitress button. "I'm also supposed to use my happy, peppy charm to get people to order apps. If you do, I swear I'll pay you back for them at school tomorrow. I'm teetering on the brink of unemployment here." Lucinda raised her voice again and stood up ramrod straight. "Or maybe you'd like to try our supercrunchy mozzarella sticks. They're yum-my!"

"Fried cheese." Maria shook her head with a grimace. "Is it just me, or is there something obscene about the whole concept of fried cheese?" She shot an evil glance at Michael, as if he was the inventor of the mozzarella stick. Clearly if Maria was wearing a button right now, the words *I'm a happy* would not be anywhere on it.

"We'll take the wings," Michael said, avoiding

Maria's gaze. "And a medium pie, one-third veggie, two-thirds meatball and pineapple. One mineral water, one Lime Warp—" He looked at Trevor.

"Orange soda," Trevor said.

"You got it!" Lucinda cried, and rushed off.

"Thanks for asking what I wanted," Maria muttered.

Michael wanted to yell at her to speak up if she expected a response. Instead he tried to be rational since she was obviously incapable.

"Maria, we've eaten here one billion times," Michael said, pulling a napkin out of the dispenser and starting to shred it in front of him. "One billion times you've eaten veggie pizza. What is the problem?"

"The problem is just because you're a guy, you think you get to make all the decisions about everything," she shot back, her eyes as bright as blue flames.

"This has nothing to do with being a guy—," Michael began, shredding faster.

Trevor cleared his throat and leaned forward in his seat. "Can we talk about our nonexistent backup plan?"

Maria ignored him. "You know I'm a vegetarian, and yet you still went ahead and ordered chicken wings," she said accusatorily.

"What? You wanted the pornographic fried cheese?" Michael demanded in a whisper.

"Obscene," Maria muttered, seeming to have forgotten how to speak in any other manner.

"When I was with DuPris, he made me watch all these old sitcoms," Trevor interjected in a matter-of-fact tone. "There was one where, I think it was Bobby and Peter, drew a line down the middle of their room. And then there was one where the Skipper and Gilligan drew a line down the middle of their hut. There was also one where Grandpa and Herman drew a line down—"

"Excuse me, but what the hell are you talking about?" Michael exploded, ripping the last of the napkin in half.

"I was thinking that maybe if I drew a line down the center of the table, and we said that half was yours and half was Maria's, then we could start working on a plan, which is why we're all here," Trevor explained, clearly irritated.

"I didn't do anything," Michael muttered, flopping back in his seat. Little pieces of napkin fluttered to the floor, and he just watched them.

"Yeah, right," Maria muttered, flopping in the exact same way.

"Max," Trevor said. He laid his hands flat on the table and looked back and forth at the two of them. "Max Evans. *Your* friend. That's why we're here, remember?"

Michael shoved his hands through his hair. Trevor was right. Time they wasted now could endanger Max later. And arguing with Maria was definitely a waste of time.

"So, what did we learn with our last, massively failed plan?" he asked.

"That connecting to the consciousness and trying to shatter it from the inside is not an option," Maria answered, her voice ultracalm. Her gaze was focused on the table.

"We also know that when we connect and use the two Stones in tandem, it doesn't give them more power," Trevor added. You could hear the relief in his tone, and he sat back slightly.

"So basically, we have squat." Michael dropped his head back on the booth and waited while Lucinda deposited the drinks and wings on the table. "Maybe we're going to have to go with DuPris's plan after all," he said when she was out of earshot again.

"But that means killing all those innocent beings," Maria protested. Still no eye contact.

"None of us want that," Trevor said, taking a sip of his soda. "But it's starting to look like it might be the only way. So much death to save one life—even Max's life—would be unthinkable. But this isn't only about Max. The consciousness must be shattered for every being that is fighting for the right to an individual life."

"If it comes to that, you won't have to do it alone," Michael told Trevor. His heart was pounding with fear, but he meant every word he said. "I'll go through the wormhole with you and help you lead the squadron on the mission to capture the other Stone."

Maria made a gasping, gurgling sound but didn't say anything. Michael got very busy pouring some sugar into the blue cheese sauce and stirring it with his finger so he wouldn't have to look at her.

He dipped a wing in the blue-cheese-and-sugar mixture, then took a bite, but he could hardly taste it because he could feel Maria's eyes on him. Reluctantly he looked up at her. God, her face was so pale—which made her raspberry lips look even more raspberryish. Even from across the table he could see how tense the muscles in her neck were. He wanted to reach over and smooth the knots out with his fingers, and—

"I have to take a leak," Michael blurted suddenly. And then he bolted. Ate one bite of a wing, and I turned into a total chicken, he thought, disgusted with himself for running away. He stomped into the men's bathroom and did a quick foot check under the stalls. Nobody.

Michael glared at himself in the nearest grungy mirror. "Face the truth. The tapering off, the Operation Cold Turkey, it wasn't just for Maria's sake. It was for yours, too. And you totally blew it last night. Now leave the girl alone. Stop even thinking about her, especially thinking about anything that involves touching."

Michael paced in a tight circle, then returned to his position in front of the mirror. "The way you feel about Maria—that's not a reason to give up the biggest dream of your life. It's not a reason to blow off helping to rebuild a freakin' *world.* It's what your parents would have wanted. You and Trevor, continuing their work together."

He leaned over and splashed some cold water on his face. "Remember Cameron?" he asked himself as he raised his dripping head back up. "Remember how you felt about her? Well, you don't really feel that way anymore. So, who knows? In a few months Maria might not even—"

Except now that he'd had some time away from Cameron, he didn't think he'd ever come close to feeling about her the way he felt about Maria. What he and Cameron went through in the compound was so intense, it formed an instant bond between them. And yeah, she was hot. But he and Maria had spent nights, and nights, and nights together, watching horror movies and baby-sitting. It was like Maria had put down roots in his body without him even noticing. Until now. Until he thought of never seeing her again.

"You've got to do this," Michael told himself, dunking his head again. "Operation Cold Turkey is in full effect." He grabbed a couple of paper towels and dried off his hair as he returned to the booth.

"The Stones are so phenomenally powerful," Maria said as he approached. "It's hard to believe there's anything two of them couldn't do." She didn't glance at Michael as he slid back into his seat.

Trevor grabbed a slice of the pizza that had been served while Michael was lecturing himself in the can.

"I'm not totally sure all three Stones are absolutely necessary to shatter the consciousness," he admitted. "It may just be that as long as the consciousness has even one of the Stones' power available to it, it will be strong enough to hold off an attack from the other two."

"That doesn't help at all, does it?" Michael said, stirring his straw in his drink. "Getting the Stone away from the consciousness isn't any easier than taking it for ourselves." He took one of the meatball-and-pineapple slices and coated it with his own personal dipping sauce.

Maria wrinkled her nose in disgust and took a long sip of her mineral water. "I wonder what kind of range that device Kyle used on the Stone has. Remember—it sucked all the power out of the Stone in seconds."

"And it took days to recharge it," Trevor added.

"There's no way it's powerful enough to reach all the way to the home planet," Michael said, taking a bite of his concoction.

"What about a timer? Or a remote?" Maria asked. She wasn't eating a thing, and Michael had a feeling his offer to Trevor was the reason, but he didn't say anything. "I just don't want you—you two—to have to go back there, and—and have all those beings die if there's another way."

Trevor dropped his slice back to his plate. "Maybe we *could* rig up a timer to that device and send it through a wormhole. It would take out the Stone at home, but the two we have would be safe."

"So, step one—we get the device," Michael said, feeling the adrenaline begin to pump through his body. This was good. They were starting to form a plan. A shoddy plan, but a plan nonetheless.

"Right," Maria said, shifting in her seat. "But only Kyle Valenti knows where it is."

"Okay, so where's Kyle?" Trevor asked, taking a huge bite of pizza.

"He's still . . . *resting,*" Maria answered. "In the mental institution."

* * *

Liz tightened her grip on Max's leg. She kept her eyes focused on Alex. If she let herself glance down at Max's body, she got the chilling feeling that she, Alex, and Isabel were his pallbearers. *He's still alive, and he's still Max,* she reassured herself. *He's just . . . hidden from you right now.*

"Watch out, Alex! You almost let his head hit the stair railing!" Isabel exclaimed.

Alex gave a grunt in reply and kept climbing backward, cradling Max's shoulders in his arms. He carefully inched through the open front door of Michael's apartment. "Do you need a break before we take him the rest of the way?"

Liz and Isabel exchanged a look. "No, we're okay. Keep going," Liz answered. Her breath was coming a little hard, but she didn't want to lay Max down on the floor like a basket of laundry that had gotten too heavy. She kicked the apartment door shut when she cleared it, and then they crept down the hallway toward the bedroom. Her arms were aching by the time they managed to put Max down on the bed, but she still hated to let him go.

"We'll look for the Stones again tomorrow," Isabel announced, in case the consciousness was listening. She brushed Max's hair off his forehead and stared down at his face for a long moment. "So, we'll be in the kitchen if you need anything. Okay, Max?"

"I want to stay in here a little bit again and just—um—visit," Liz stammered. She adjusted her backpack, feeling her supplies slide around inside.

"Leave the door open. And don't get too close, okay?" Alex said.

Liz nodded, even though she knew she had absolutely no intention of following Alex's instructions. As soon as he and Isabel were safely in the kitchen, Liz closed the door halfway, figuring one of them would come check on her if she shut it completely, and sat down on the edge of the bed next to Max.

"I've been reading this book on comas," she told him. "I know you're not in one, but I thought some of the experimental techniques they've tried to bring coma patients back to consciousness might work on you." She pulled off her backpack and unzipped it, watching Max's face the entire time. "The big thing seems to be stimulating the senses, through methods like music or even pain. But don't worry, there will be no pain involved," Liz added quickly.

Oh, God. Did I blow it? Did I just announce to the consciousness my whole plan and give it time to defend itself? But it was too late to worry about that now. She took a CD out of her backpack, stuck it in the player on the nightstand, selected the track, and hit play.

"Remember this one?" she asked, focusing on Max's eyes. "It's the song that was playing during our dance as homecoming queen and king, our first dance together." Her heart squeezed as she listened to the melody and remembered how she felt that night—beautiful and special and loved. She tried to push the feelings aside.

"You were so surprised you'd won, I wasn't sure

you'd even be able to move. But it was a great dance."

Liz stopped talking and let the music fill the room. As she listened, she could almost see the cheesy yellow and brown crepe paper streamers that had filled the gym that night, could almost see the shock in Max's bright blue eyes when she'd pretty much asked him to kiss her, shock followed by warmth that had almost melted her bones.

Was the song flooding Max with images the way it was her? Or was the consciousness now controlling the part of Max's brain that held his memories? His face gave her no clue. There was no change of expression.

"Okay, let's try something else," Liz said when the song ended. She snapped off the CD player and removed a bottle of ketchup from her backpack. The smell always brought her back to one of the most intense experiences of her life. She thought it might do the same for Max.

"Worth a shot," she mumbled as she turned Max's palm up, smoothing out his fingers. She touched him a little longer than she needed to, then upended the bottle and waited for a dollop to fall onto his skin.

"Come on, come on." She gave the side of the bottle an impatient smack. Then, remembering the trick her mama had taught her, she found the little raised 57 on the glass and hit the bottle again, right over the number. With a plop a blob of ketchup fell into Max's hand. Liz curled his fingers over and rubbed them in it. "Remember ketchup?" she asked. "You broke a ketchup bottle and poured it over my stomach to cover the blood, remember, Max? It was the day you healed me. The day you saved my life."

Max's face remained blank. Liz ran one of her fingers through the ketchup and then held it under his nose. "Remember that day, Max? The day everything changed? The day you risked everything for me?"

It's not working, she realized. Something else. Something else. Liz wiped off her finger and Max's hand, then rooted through her backpack frantically. She'd really thought the ketchup was a great choice, but just because that smell always jerked her back to that wonderful, horrible moment didn't mean it was the trigger for Max.

"Maybe this will work for you," Liz said. She pulled free a dark green dress, lace over a lighter, silky smooth layer, then ran the cloth down Max's cheek. "This was what I was wearing when I told you I loved you the very first time. Remember?" She rubbed the cloth against his skin again, harder. Too hard. The lace made a row of tiny scratches.

"Oh, sorry." Liz kissed her fingers, then pressed them over the scratches. "Sorry," she repeated, kissing the scratches themselves.

She scooted closer to Max, and the backpack fell onto the floor. She didn't bother to pick it up. When she'd been gathering all the items that might snap Max back to her, she'd forgotten about the physical sensation that, at least for her, was more powerful than anything else—a kiss.

Liz knew the consciousness could be feeling

everything that she was doing to Max and that he might not be aware of any of it. But she pushed that thought out of her mind.

"I love you, Max," she said, clearly and forcefully. Then she lowered her head and kissed him, trying to infuse the kiss with all the emotion and passion she had inside her—that she had inside her for *Max*.

His lips were cool, and still, and dead feeling, but Liz didn't pull away. I love you, she thought. Can't you feel that? Remember? *Remember?*

A hand wrapped itself in her hair. Another hand pressed itself against her back, urging her closer, closer, closer. Without breaking the kiss, Liz opened her eyes and looked into Max's eyes—bright and aware and full of love.

She pulled back just enough to speak. "Oh, God, Max. You're all right!"

"Maybe Alex knew what he was talking about when he called me Snow White," he said, his voice thick. "I just needed the right kiss."

"You heard that?" Liz exclaimed. Then she kissed him again before he could answer, starving for the taste of him, wishing she could swallow him, absorb him, make him a part of her or become a part of him.

"Yeah, I heard that," Max answered finally, breathless. "I heard everything. But . . . I'd given up trying to fight my way back. I was too deep. It was too far. Then I felt you kissing me. And I just—"

He rolled her underneath him, stretching his body over hers. "Liz, there's so much I want to say. Need to say. About Adam. About how you were right about the consciousness all along. But I can't stop. . . ." His mouth was on hers, desperate and fierce.

Liz locked one of her legs over his, then slid both her hands under his shirt so she could feel his skin. Closer. She wanted to be even closer.

"Max," she gasped, speaking his name against his lips.

Suddenly his mouth went slack. It slipped away from hers, and Max's head fell against Liz's shoulder as if all the muscles in his neck had been cut.

"Max!" Liz shouted. "Max!" His motionless body pinned her to the mattress, pressing down on her until she thought her heart and lungs would cease to function. "Max!" she screamed again.

Suddenly she was free. She sat up and found Alex and Isabel pulling Max to the other side of the bed. "What happened?" Alex demanded. "Did he attack you?"

"No." Liz shoved herself to her feet. "That's not . . ." She raised her fingers to her lips. They were still warm from Max's. "He kissed me."

TEN

Don't even think about demanding to know the exact meaning of "I'm thinking about it," Maria ordered herself. Don't even think about begging to know if he's going to go or if he's going to stay. She stared out at the straight stretch of highway leading to Albuquerque, not allowing herself even a sidelong, superfast peek at Michael. She could feel the questions on her tongue, crouched down, waiting to leap out.

No. No, no, no, she thought. Remember the last time you decided to hand Michael an ultimatum—choose between me and Isabel right here, right now? Remember what a babbling, stammering, sweating hunk of patheticness you were that day? And remember how you so did not like what you heard? You were positive you'd feel better if you could just make Michael say something concrete. But you were wrong. Wrong to the power of infinity. So learn from your past mistakes. Even rats in mazes can learn from their mistakes, and so can you. Keep your mouth shut.

Maria locked her teeth together. She crossed her legs. She crossed her arms. She tightened her muscles, using all her strength and will to not speak.

"Do you need to stop?" Michael asked, not even looking at her. "There's a gas station in a couple of miles, I think."

"Mmm-mmm," Maria answered, shaking her head. She didn't dare to allow herself any actual words.

"Are you sure?" he pressed.

"I'm not a toddler. I know if I have to pee or not, Michael, all right?" she blurted out. She clamped her teeth back together hard—and caught a tiny piece of her tongue between them. Do not attempt to speak again, she told herself. She'd felt this sucking sensation when she'd opened her mouth to make the pee announcement. If she hadn't gotten her lips together as fast as she had, a whole flood of words would have come rushing out. It would not have been pretty.

Maria scrunched her jean jacket into a ball, propped it against the window, and rested her head on it. She wasn't kidding herself. She knew that there was no chance she'd fall asleep. But pretending to fall asleep would make it easier to keep the dam of her teeth closed tight against the words.

She concentrated on keeping her breathing slow and even, which was the best way of appearing really zonked out, but for some reason the slower she breathed, the harder her heart pounded, slamming painfully against her ribs. It felt like it was trying to escape, to say the words she wouldn't allow her lips and tongue to form—Michael, what in the holy hell does "I'm thinking about it" mean?

Are you going? Are you staying? And what about *me?*

"We're here," Michael announced. Maria only opened her eyes after the car came to a complete stop, then she scrambled out of the passenger door and started toward the main entrance of the Bradley Institute without waiting for Michael.

She rushed inside and over to the front desk. "I—we're—here to see Kyle Valenti," she said breathlessly, trying to concentrate on something other than the possibility that Michael was going to be living in another galaxy in the near future.

"That's nice," the nurse answered with a way-too-big smile. "Kyle hasn't had many visitors. Just his aunt." She pushed a clipboard toward Maria. "I just need you to sign here."

Maria did, then moved farther down the counter so Michael had room to sign as well. She caught a glimpse of his hands as he wrote and wished she hadn't. Just looking at them made her think about all kinds of things she didn't want to think about. Like the way they felt tangled in her hair. Or stroking her back. Not that his hands had been doing anything like that in a long time.

"I'll buzz you in," the nurse said, pulling Maria away from her thoughts. "Kyle's in the common room. It's the second door to the left."

Michael continued to trail along behind her, which wasn't exactly like him. Apparently he wasn't all that eager to talk to her, either. But why? *She* wasn't the one who was planning on deserting *him*.

"This is the second door," Michael announced from behind her.

"I knew that." Maria spun around and marched back down the hall to the second door. Michael opened it for her like she was some kind of invalid or something, and she strode through. She scanned the room and saw Kyle and a couple of older men parked on a ratty couch in front of the tube.

"Kyle," she blurted out, her voice sounding oddly loud in the large room.

Kyle looked up, but he didn't seem very excited to have visitors. He shoved himself to his feet and headed over to them.

"What?" he demanded.

"How have you been?" Maria said, suddenly nervous and wishing she'd thought to bring him some candy or something. Kyle wasn't one of her favorite people, but nobody should have to live in a place like this. It was clean, and the nurse had seemed friendly and all, but the place smelled . . . depressing. There was too much Pine Sol filling the air.

"You did not come here to find out how I've been," Kyle answered, voice flat. He crossed his arms over his chest and glared at her. Maria had to concentrate to keep from taking a step back.

"The guy who killed your father is dead," Michael said, voice low and intense.

A flash of emotion—pain, anger, sorrow—burst across Kyle's face, then he tightened his lips and stared at them expressionlessly. "You didn't come here to tell me that, either. You want something."

"You're right. I'm not going to try to feed you a load of bull," Michael answered. "We need the device—the one you used on the Stone that day."

"Oh, sure. I have it right here in my pocket," Kyle said sarcastically.

"This is important, Kyle," Maria told him, looking him in the eye. "Life and death."

"Well, Liz should have thought about whether or not you would need me for anything before she got me shipped here," Kyle answered.

"Liz didn't—," Maria protested.

"Like hell she didn't," Kyle interrupted. "I got put on the express train to squirrelville the same day Liz told those reporters I hadn't been *myself* since my dad died. Coincidence? I don't think so."

"What do you want, Valenti?" Michael demanded in a harsh whisper. "Money?"

Kyle laughed, a laugh that went on way too long. Maybe the kid did belong in a loony bin. "Yeah. They have a great mall in here."

"Then what?" Michael asked. Maria noticed his hands curling into fists. She wrapped her fingers around his arm, silently warning him not to lose his temper and trying to ignore the heat she could feel seeping from Michael's body into hers.

"Oh, gosh. It looks like it's time for my meds." Kyle jerked his chin toward another nurse, who had begun moving through the room with a tray of little paper cups. "You'll have to excuse me." He turned on his heel and walked away, leaving Maria and Michael staring after him helplessly.

"We never should have sent Michael and Maria to get information from Kyle," Isabel told Trevor, tucking a stray blond hair behind her ear as she perched on the edge of her bed. "Neither of them has the necessary finesse."

"And you do?" Trevor asked teasingly, causing her to blush. Isabel found she liked being teased by him, which was somewhat unusual. It put him in a very small and very select group.

She put on her haughtiest look. "Don't you ever doubt it. I drip finesse," she answered.

"Ooh. That's attractive," Trevor shot back.

Isabel laughed, stretching out flat on her back on her comforter. "Give me a few minutes in Kyle's dream orb, and we'll have the exact location of the device. Then we'll be so close to getting Max back."

Trevor stood up from her desk chair. "Should I go?" he asked, suddenly sounding sort of shy in an adorable little-boy way.

"No, it's okay." Isabel closed her eyes, pleasantly aware of Trevor's eyes on her. She turned her head slightly, allowing her blond hair to fan out on her pillow. Pretty picture, huh, Trevor? she thought. Then she began tensing her muscles and relaxing them in sequence, from her feet all the way up to her neck. Tense, relax. Tense, relax. Her body went all soft and pliant, and the swirling orbs of the dream plane became clear in all their shimmering glory.

So beautiful. Isabel let out a sigh of pleasure. There hadn't been enough beauty in her life lately because she'd been so worried about Max. But she had a feeling deep in her gut that their latest plan was going to work. Liz had proved that Max could still respond, that he wasn't completely and totally controlled by the consciousness, at least not every moment. When they used the device to shatter the consciousness, Isabel was sure her brother would find a way to help. And to free himself.

One of the dream orbs whirled closer, brushing soft as a soap bubble against Isabel's cheek. She recognized the orb. It belonged to Tish Okabe, one of her closest friends—outside the tight circle of those who knew the secret. Isabel allowed herself a moment to appreciate the iridescent whirls of color in Tish's orb, then began to hum, coaxing the dream orb that belonged to Kyle toward her.

It responded almost immediately, whipping toward her bullet fast and spinning to a stop in her outstretched hands.

"Eager, aren't you?" she whispered, then slowly spread her hands apart, urging the dream orb to expand. Soon it was large enough to step inside, but Isabel took a moment to survey the dream from without.

She felt a twinge of pity when she saw that Kyle was dreaming about being in the institution. The guy couldn't even get out of there for a couple of hours when he was asleep. Well, she could give him one pleasant association with the place—while she was getting what she wanted.

"I think you'll like this, Kyle," she said. An instant later she was dressed in a nurse's uniform, a very short, very tight nurse's uniform. Her hair was in a French twist, with a few tendrils free around her face. "I think you'll like this a lot." With a satisfied smile she stepped through the wall of Kyle's dream orb.

"Time for your shoulder rub," she said, all bright and perky as she headed toward the single bed in the dreary room. "Sit up, please." Kyle eagerly obeyed, and Isabel sat down on the bed beside him, taking a moment to turn the sheets from rough cotton to perfumed satin. She began massaging his shoulders, sometimes leaning close enough for her breasts to almost brush against him. Almost.

"I need to ask you a few questions. For your chart," Isabel announced, keeping up the massage. "Can you describe one of your fantasies for me?"

"This is pretty much at the top of the list," Kyle answered. He had to clear his throat a few times before he got it out.

"Uh-huh. Interesting," Isabel answered. She also thought it was interesting how people would accept pretty much anything in a dream. She hadn't changed her face or anything, but Kyle didn't seem to think there was anything strange about Isabel Evans turning up as his nurse.

"And what's your favorite color? I'm very curious about that." Isabel moved the massage a little lower down Kyle's back.

"Blue. Like your eyes," Kyle answered immediately, needing to clear his throat a few times for that one, too.

"Mmm-hmm." Isabel moved the massage still lower, getting a sound that was part gasp and part yelp from Kyle. "And that device that you used on the Stone. Where is that now?"

"Guys' bathroom closest to the cafeteria." Kyle half spoke, half groaned. "Metal box. Taped behind the toilet. Last stall."

"Good boy." Isabel patted him on the head. "I'm sure you'll be out of here real soon. Just stop talking about aliens. That's just silly."

And she was outta there. Out of the orb and out of the dream plane. "Finesse, that's all it takes," she said to Trevor as she opened her eyes. "The device is at school. We'll get there early and pick it up."

Trevor stood up. "Good job," he said. He backed two steps toward the door, then immediately took a step forward, toward her. "It's almost time for the two hours' sleep. I should change back to Max and go to my room." He took another step closer to Isabel.

"Yeah, you probably should," she answered, teasing Trevor a little even though, being a guy, he didn't realize he was being teased.

Trevor got a deer-in-the-headlights, Dawson-ish

look on his face. "Uh, I talked to Michael, and if we shatter the consciousness, he's going back home with me," he blurted out.

Isabel felt like she'd been stabbed in the heart, but Trevor didn't give her a second to recover from that little bombshell before he hit her with another.

"I want you to go with us," he added. Then he stumbled forward, sat down on the bed, and kissed her. All his clumsiness disappeared as soon as his lips touched hers.

This has to be his first kiss in his human form. And he's already so good at it, she thought fuzzily. Then she stopped thinking, all her attention needed just to *feel*. Feel his tongue brushing against hers, feel his hand curving around her neck, feel the heat of him as he pulled her closer.

"Wow," she mumbled when he finally released her. And Isabel wasn't a girl who said *wow*. Her heart was pounding as if she'd just run a mile.

"Do you think you would want to come back with me?" Trevor asked throatily. "Is it a possibility at all?"

Isabel smoothed her hair away from her face, trying to give her brain a few seconds to get fully functional again.

"I . . . I think I need to wait and see what happens with Max," she answered. "He might not be in great shape when we break him free."

Trevor stood up and met her gaze, his eyes serious. "Iz, I want you to be prepared. I don't think—I really don't think you should be assuming that Max is going to make it."

Another stabbing pain, this one in her heart *and* her gut. "I'm really tired," she said shortly, standing. "I'll talk to you in the morning. Remember, we have to be at school early to get the device."

She wanted him out of there, and she approached the door, forcing him to walk out ahead of her. As long as he stood in her room, his words would continue to hang over her head, waiting to fall, waiting to crush her.

"Isabel, I—"

"Just go, Trevor," she said. Then, seeing the hurt look on his face, she forced a tight smile. "Please. I'm really tired."

She didn't let a single tear fall until the door was closed behind him.

"I cut school and started working on the timer," Trevor told the group.

Michael leaned across his kitchen table and studied the silver disk in Trevor's hand. "When will you have it ready to go?" he asked.

"It won't take much longer," Trevor answered, turning the disk over and over in his hand. "Isabel's going to help me wrap it up and hook up a remote so we can guide the device at least partway through the wormhole. We should be finished late tonight."

"So tomorrow morning we do this thing," Michael said, glancing from Isabel to Trevor to Liz to Alex, but keeping his eyes away from Maria. He'd started having a hard time looking at her. It had gotten to the point where it actually hurt to see her face.

"Is there anything we should be doing?" Alex asked, leaning his elbows on the table.

Trevor shook his head. "Getting the timer and the remote hooked up is a two-person job. And that's all there is to do."

"That and get through tonight," Liz said. She twisted her hair into a knot on top of her head, then immediately let it fall free. "The waiting is driving me crazy."

Get through tonight, Michael thought. How was he going to do that? This could be his last night on earth. He shouldn't waste it watching TV. Without a conscious decision, Michael's eyes went to Maria. She was pale . . . and beautiful. He felt something wrench inside his body and looked away fast.

"I'm—I've got some stuff to do. Stay here as long as you want." He made his escape, slamming out the door and pounding down the staircase leading to the parking lot. As soon as his feet hit asphalt, he started to run. He kept running until he got to the doughnut shop.

Yeah. This is definitely a last-night-on-earth kind of event, he thought as he stepped inside and pulled in his first breath of the sugary air. He couldn't take off without having a few more of his crullers.

Michael ordered himself an even dozen, then sat down at his usual table and pulled a handful of hot sauce packets out of his jacket pocket. He got one of the crullers set up just the way he liked it and took a big bite.

It tasted like dust. He added more hot sauce and took another bite. More dust.

Michael finished off the cruller, then ate two more, pretending they actually tasted good to him, then he shoved away his tray. Now what? A last trip to the mall? A last slice of Flying Pepperoni pizza? A last trip to Adam's grave to tell him that he was leaving?

He picked up one of the uneaten crullers and twisted it with both hands until it broke into sticky chunks. There was no question about where he wanted to go. Right now he wanted to be holed up in Maria's girlie-girl room, doing . . . anything. Watching some bad horror movie. Anything. As long as she was there doing it with him.

But that's not going to happen, he ordered himself. It's not fair to her. And be honest, buddy, it would probably kill you.

ELEVEN

Isabel nervously twirled a golf club between her fingers, scanning the parking lot of the Black Hole Putt-Putt Golf Course. She smiled when she spotted Alex's VW Rabbit turning in, then rushed over to the car as he pulled into a parking spot. Isabel didn't make a habit of rushing toward guys—even if she felt like it. But there was no reason to play those kinds of games with Alex.

"I got you a golf club already," she announced before Alex even had a chance to swing both feet to the ground.

"Thanks," Alex said. He took one of the clubs and shook his head, laughing.

"What?" Isabel asked, grinning because his laugh was always contagious.

"I was just thinking about the last time we came here," he answered. "My brain was doing this gerbil-on-an-exercise-wheel thing. I kept trying to figure out if you thought we were on a date, or, you know, some kind of significant outing. And I was obsessed with debating whether or not you could actually want me to touch you."

"I bet you almost had a heart attack when I kissed you," Isabel said, nudging him with her club. "Remember? It was right over—"

Alex grabbed her hand and pulled her halfway across the parking lot. "It was right here," he told her. He pointed toward a small, spray-painted *X*. "I put that there," he admitted.

Coming from someone else, this gesture might have seemed odd, but coming from Alex, Isabel didn't even blink. "I can't believe how much has happened since then. How much has changed." Isabel knelt down and gently touched the *X*.

"As Liz's dad would say, what a long, strange trip it's been," Alex answered. "So when are you going to get around to telling me whatever it is you want to tell me? Because I'm just not going for your story about having an irresistible desire to play minigolf."

"Trevor didn't need me after all," Isabel said, standing, but finding herself unable to meet his eyes. "It turned out that the two-person job was more of a one-person job. I just wanted to get out of the house and—" Isabel stopped herself, blushing. "All right, I do need to talk to you," she confessed.

"Father Manes is ready to listen," he said, lowering his voice. He led the way to the first hole.

Isabel carefully positioned her ball on the little rubber mat, stalling, then straightened up and gave the ball a whack without even trying to aim at one of the moon craters.

"Here's the deal. After we shatter the consciousness—" She didn't allow herself even a mental *if*. "After we shatter it, Michael is going to go back to the home planet with Trevor to help rebuild the society.

Of course, Michael hasn't bothered to tell me or anyone else. I heard all this from Trevor. It's just like when Michael would change foster homes. He'd hardly even say a word about it."

Alex hit his ball down the faded purple carpet. His didn't get through one of the moon craters, either. "This is . . . it's big."

"That's not all," Isabel told him. She wanted to get everything out, needed to, but her hands were getting sweaty and her heart was pounding. "Trevor asked me to go with them. And I just have no idea what I should do. I was making myself insane, then I realized that I needed to talk it over with someone." She shook her head. "No. I needed to talk it over with *you*. I knew you'd help me figure out what I should do."

"Are you two golfing or what?" a kid yelled from behind them.

"Hey, pip-squeak. This is a serious game. For serious people. You can't respect that, I suggest you leave," Alex said. He took Isabel's hand and led her down the fairway, grabbing both their balls and throwing them into the moon crater. A few seconds later they clunked into the metal cup on the other side. "That's two holes in two. Write that down with one of those little pencils," he told her. Then he led the way over to a bench by a shocking pink spaceship. "So, what are you thinking?" he asked.

"I'm thinking . . ." Isabel gave a helpless shrug. "I don't know what I'm thinking."

"I'm not saying you should go, but it would be

kind of like living in *Star Wars,*" Alex said. "I always wanted to live in *Star Wars.*"

"Where everyone has long hair and gold bikinis?" Isabel chided.

"Not *everyone,*" Alex said, sounding horrified. "Only the women." He waved the group of kids past them. "We're considering the strategy of the next hole. You can play through." He turned his attention back to Isabel. "That's only part of my *Star Wars* fascination. I just always thought it would be cool to be part of something so important."

"So you want to save the universe, surrounded by girls in gold bikinis," Isabel commented.

"Exactly. So many times I've felt like my life is so little and insignificant. And I daydream about having the chance to do something—dork alert!—heroic. Like Han Solo," Alex admitted, a faint blush coloring his cheeks. "Then when I found out the truth about you and the others, it's almost like I got the chance. This year we've had to deal with a lot of life-and-death stuff. Sometimes I wonder how it's going to feel to go back to freaking about zits on my back or whatever."

"Shopping for the perfect accessories," Isabel added. She stretched her legs out in front of her. "I don't think I'll ever find anything more meaningful to do with my life than help the beings who fought against the collective consciousness."

She didn't usually spend a lot of time thinking about meaning-of-life-type issues. It seemed like a waste. But that's what this decision was really about. Isabel had the chance to be a part of something enormous—the restructuring of a whole planet. Her real home.

"And the downside is?" Alex asked, raising his eyebrows.

"It would ruin my parents' lives," Isabel answered. She didn't even need a second to think about that one. "I'd just disappear. And they'd never stop looking for me, wondering if I was alive or dead. It's different for Michael. All the people that really matter to him know the truth. They'll at least know what happened. And he'll have his brother with him."

"You'd have Michael with you," Alex said. "And Trevor." He turned and watched the kids finish up the spaceship hole. "I get the feeling something may be starting between the two of you," he added, without looking at her.

"Maybe," Isabel agreed. "But I'm not going to go live on another planet because I like the way a guy kisses." Although there was more than kisses between her and Trevor. They'd known each other such a short time, but there was this *comfort* between them.

"The editors of *Ms.* magazine will be glad to hear it," Alex said, still looking at the kids.

Isabel reached out, took his chin in her fingers, and turned his head toward her. "It's okay that I'm talking to you about Trevor, isn't it?"

Alex met her gaze steadily. "Yeah. I get a little . . . *ping,* I guess you'd call it," he said with a shrug. "But it's just your basic guy jealousy crap. I mean, we're friends, Isabel. And I—dork alert again—I love you as a friend. I want you to have everything you want. Including Trevor if that's the way it goes down."

"I love you, too," Isabel answered. "And there's nothing dorky about it. God, I would miss you so much if I went. You, and Maria, and Liz. And it's not like I could just call you up if I needed to hear your voice. I couldn't even send my parents a Christmas card."

"When is all this supposed to happen?" Alex asked, looking away again. "When are Trevor and Michael going to go back?"

"They're going to use the wormhole we open to send the device," Isabel answered.

"So tomorrow." Alex sounded a little dazed.

Isabel knew how he was feeling. How could she make a decision about the rest of her life in less than a day?

"I told Trevor I needed to see how Max was first," Isabel said, following Alex's gaze out over the golf course. "If he needs me, I'm staying. That's it."

"But if Max comes through okay . . ." Alex let his sentence trail off.

Isabel took a deep breath and sighed. "Then . . . then I might end up going."

Stop! Maria ordered her feet. Stop right there.

But her feet kept walking as if they had minds of their own—walking back toward the museum, even though she'd only left the place a few hours before.

"Turn around," she pleaded, feeling so desperate, she was willing to be seen talking to her feet on a public sidewalk. The feet didn't obey. Step by step by step, they kept taking her closer to the museum. To Michael.

Her feet marched her across the UFO parking lot, then straight up the stairs. Maria's hand seemed to have its own brain, too. It opened the apartment door, without knocking, and then the feet moved her straight inside.

Just because I'm here doesn't mean I have to say anything I don't want to say, she thought. I can just tell Michael I thought I left my jacket over here or something. Then I'll just leave. If my demonic feet will let me.

Michael stepped out of the kitchen, and Maria's heart hit her throat. He looked at her like she was the very last person on earth he wanted to see. "Thought I heard someone come in."

Maria's feet walked her right over to him, not stopping until there were only a few inches separating her from him. He took a step back. The feet took a step forward. Okay, ask about the jacket, she told herself.

"Tell me the exact, precise, Michael-Webster-dictionary definition of 'I'm thinking about it,'" she demanded, her voice coming out loud and defiant. Oh, God. Her mouth was possessed, too.

"What?" Michael asked, his voice low.

"Don't pull any crap, Michael. We both know exactly what I'm asking you. Are you going? Or are you staying? Tell me. Right here. Right now," Maria insisted.

I didn't mean to say that! I didn't want to say that! she silently wailed.

Michael went into his usual lockdown mode, giving no indication of what he was thinking or feeling. "Look, I'm not asking for much. What I want is information. And if you're leaving, I want a good-bye. You owe me that much," Maria continued.

She didn't know who she was channeling. But whoever it was, Maria was starting to like her. Michael did owe her a good-bye. He couldn't just disappear from her life as if . . . as if they barely knew each other.

Michael hesitated, silence filling the room all around them. All the power and fight evaporated from Maria's body. Suddenly she was in control of her feet again. And her mouth. Whatever Michael was going to say to her, she was going to have to hear without whatever force had gotten her this far.

"Good-bye." Michael's voice was flat. His eyes were on hers, but there was no hint of emotion in their gray depths. Not anger. Not sadness. Nothing. Something died inside Maria.

"Good-bye," she repeated. "That's it?"

"That's what you said you wanted," he answered. "What did you expect? You know I've been trying to find a way home my whole life. And the rebellion—my parents were part of that."

His parents. Maria hadn't even thought of that. His parents had been part of the Kindred, and his brother was part of it now. Joining the group was Michael's chance at feeling like part of a family.

"Why couldn't you say that to me before?" she

asked. "If you cared about me even a little, tiny bit, you would have come out and—"

Maria stopped herself. What was the point? She was his friend. Someone he might miss a little. Someone he might think about once in a while. But she wasn't vital to him. Not like he was to her. He was her oxygen. Her water. Her sustenance. And she was his friend. *Friend.* What a weak, pathetic word that was.

"Maria, you know I—," Michael began.

"See you tomorrow." Maria couldn't deal with listening to him try to come up with something nice to say to her. *Nice.* Another weak, pathetic word. She spun around and raced for the door. Then she flew down the steps. About halfway to the ground, she stumbled. One of her feet slid on the stairs, and she fell sideways, hard.

Agony erupted in her ankle. For a moment all Maria could do was squeeze her eyes shut and let the pain wash through her. Then she grabbed the stair rail with one hand and used her other hand to straighten her leg. When she thought she could stand without screaming, she carefully limped down the remaining stairs.

Maria knew all she had to do was call up to Michael. He'd come down and heal her. That was the kind of thing you did for a *friend*. But if he did that, he'd have to make a connection with her, and Maria couldn't bear to expose her soul to him. She wasn't sure she could live through that.

* * *

"Everyone strapped in?" Trevor asked. He and Michael had rigged a bunch of safety harnesses against the back wall of the museum. The force of the wormhole was so strong, it could suck them all in if they weren't careful. He got a yes from everyone but Liz.

"I want to stay upstairs with Max," she said.

"Someone should be with him," Isabel agreed, shooting Liz a grateful look.

"I don't think there'll be anything you can do," Trevor cautioned. He didn't want her to get her hopes up. Hers or Isabel's. The chances of Max surviving the shattering of the consciousness weren't good, although Trevor didn't know for sure what would happen to *any* of the beings.

"There's nothing I can do down here, either, though, right?" Liz asked, sounding a little desperate.

"Right," Trevor answered. The plan was either going to work or it wasn't. None of them had much control over the situation. He wished they did. This was the most important day of his life, the day the beings could begin to live in freedom, no longer forced to choose between going into hiding or becoming a part of the massive monster that was the consciousness.

"We're opening up the hole pretty much right under the kitchen. If the force gets too strong in the bedroom, go low. Just flatten yourself to the floor," Michael told her.

Liz nodded. "Well . . . good luck," she said. It seemed like she wanted to say something more, but she just turned and headed for the spiral staircase that led up to Michael's apartment.

"See you afterward, at the postshattering bash," Alex called after her. "Remember, it's formal!"

"Okay, plan review," Michael said. "I'm using one of the Stones to open up the wormhole. Then Trevor's sending in the device. When it's close enough to the home planet—but far enough from here—he detonates it."

"The remote will tell me if the Stone on my planet has been drained of power," Trevor added. "If the indicator light goes from green to red, we're in business."

"Then Trevor and I both use a Stone to shoot power through the hole. We'll blast away until there's no juice left," Michael concluded.

"And then we wait," Isabel said, her voice strong even though there were wells of fear behind her eyes.

"And then we hope," Maria added.

Hope. It was pretty much all they had.

Michael pulled his Stone from his pocket. Trevor positioned the device in one hand and the remote in the other. He felt his pocket to make sure his Stone was still there, even though he knew it was.

"Here goes," Michael announced. He held the Stone out in front of him. Immediately it began to glow with its green-purple light. The light intensified until it was impossible for Trevor to look straight at it.

The museum went totally silent. Trevor didn't think anyone was even breathing. He knew *he* wasn't. Then he heard it, the soft sucking sound that indicated the hole was beginning to open. He pulled some air into his aching lungs.

We're on our way, he thought. He peered up at the ceiling, blinking away the green and purple dots that looking at the Stone had put in his vision. Yeah. There was a spot that was sort of drooping, almost oozing.

The soft patch of ceiling drooped lower. And then lower. The plaster stretched until it was as thin as a sheet of plastic wrap and almost as transparent. Trevor waited until the spot was absolutely clear. Then, with his human body pumping a stream of sweat all the way down his back, he clicked on the remote and used it to guide the device into the wormhole. The device flew up through the hole in the ceiling so fast, Trevor couldn't even track it.

He turned to look at Michael. Together they began to count. "One, one thousand; two, one thousand; three, one thousand . . ."

When they reached twenty, it was time. Trevor hit the button on the remote that would detonate the device. Then he stared at the indicator light. I want to see red here, Trevor thought urgently. Give me some red.

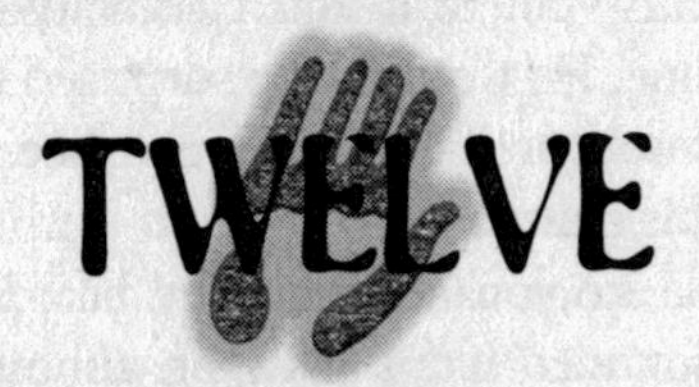

TWELVE

Michael could feel his cheeks rippling from the force of the wormhole as the straps of the safety harness cut into his chest and stomach.

"Still green?" he shouted to Trevor. His brother was only a foot away from him, but the horrible sucking sound of the open hole made it almost impossible to hear anything else.

"Still green," Trevor yelled back.

Crap. Shouldn't it have gone to red by now? What if the whole thing was a bust? Oh, just shut the hell up, he ordered himself. He forced his head to turn toward Trevor, fighting the pull of the wormhole. His brother's eyes were intent on the remote. Michael couldn't see the indicator light, but it didn't matter. Watching Trevor was just as effective. When Michael saw relief flood Trevor's face, he knew what had happened even before Trevor let out a triumphant cry of, "Red!"

Show time. Michael pointed his Stone into the wormhole and let it rip, full strength. The purple-green light flared around him in a huge circle. It was all he could see. It was almost as if he started to *become* the light. His body began to feel like pure, pulsing energy—all heat and electricity—instead of flesh and bone. He wouldn't be surprised if he started to glow himself or if his veins had been converted into wires, his neurons into circuits.

"Michael, are you all right?" he heard Isabel ask. Her voice sounded like a whisper, although Michael was sure she was screaming her lungs out. "Michael, can you answer me?" she whispered again.

The name Michael sounded strange to him. Almost meaningless. How could he answer her? He was a conduit. He'd thought maybe his body was becoming filled with wires, but now he realized his whole body *was* one big wire. Its only function was to allow the power of the Stone to surge into the wormhole. Michael felt less alive and more alive than he ever had, all at once.

"Will we know when it happens?" Alex shout whispered.

Michael didn't attempt to answer. He didn't even know the answer. He let the energy slam through him, shoving away any impulse to resist. His legs began to twitch, then his arms, then his fingers. His eyelids fluttered. And he felt his hair stand on end. Then his heart began to beat erratically, stuttering, almost stopping, stuttering again.

Was he even still holding on to the Stone? He couldn't feel it in his hand. He couldn't feel his hand at all. But he couldn't have dropped it, or the power would have stopped pounding through him.

Michael tried to tighten his fingers around the

Stone. If he let it go now, it could destroy the plan. Had his fingers moved? Had the message made its way from his brain? He had no way of knowing.

"Need help holding it," he managed to gasp out.

He was sure no one had been able to hear him, but a moment later he felt an Isabel infusion in the blast of power. It added a delicate flavor to the energy, very faint, but distinct.

"Alex, help Trevor," Isabel cried, her voice still sounding so soft.

"Got it," Alex answered.

Michael felt the power slacken slightly. The ball of purple-green light around him grew the tiniest bit less brilliant. He could feel his bones inside him again, although they felt as insubstantial as jelly.

The power of the Stone is starting to run out, he realized. And the consciousness hadn't shattered. At least he didn't think it had. They would have to be able to feel the impact of something that cataclysmic coming at them through the hole. Wouldn't they?

The purple-green light faded some more. Michael could see the hole again. They'd battened down the museum as well as they could, but one of the display cases was spinning around in midair, getting sucked into the hole. A mobile of the universe was right behind it, planets jerking wildly on their wires.

Michael reached out and grabbed Trevor's wrist. He had complete control over his own body again, although he had to strain against the pressure of the wormhole. Instantly a connection formed between him and his brother. He could feel Alex in the connection. And Maria.

Very faintly he heard the music of their connection begin, lacking something without Max and Liz. Without Adam. But still something that Michael could feel with a physical force. He pulled in a deep breath, taking in the perfume of their combined connection scents, feeling more strength return to him.

Alex threw out an image of a runner bursting through a finish line. Michael threw the image right back at him, following it up with as much energy as he could pull out of himself. Isabel zapped it out again. Then Maria. Then Trevor. Then Alex again. Then Michael. Until there was a whole marathon of runners crashing through the tape together. United. Strong. Winners.

"On three," he shouted. "One. Two. Three." They combined the power of their connection with the fading power of the Stones, and the sound of a billion voices filled the air. The voices *became* the air. Became the ground under Michael's feet, the wall behind his back. Those voices became the world. Michael couldn't make out any individual words. They were all in a language he didn't understand.

But he understood the emotions. There was fear. And fury. And relief. And joy.

"Elvis has left the building," a voice said in his ear, a voice filled with warmth. It was Ray. Michael could feel Ray's aura briefly blending with his, although he couldn't see it, in a final good-bye.

Then two new auras wrapped themselves around Michael's. There was no anger in them. And although he could feel a trace of sorrow, the overwhelming emotion that filled Michael was love—of being loved by these two beings he'd never met.

"Our parents," Trevor said. But Michael would have known that even if Trevor hadn't spoken. Michael wanted to soak up every bit of this feeling, keep it with him forever. He closed his eyes and realized there were tears on his lashes.

"Don't go," he whispered when he felt the two auras begin to slip away from his. He heard a few of the strange words in his ears, felt the love intensify until he felt like a little bit of it had been burned into his heart. Then the auras were gone. Another good-bye.

Michael's eyes snapped open as a thought exploded into his brain. Where was Max? Oh, God, where was Max? Was Michael going to feel his aura next? Was that going to be the last good-bye?

Liz stretched out on top of Max, pinning his body to the floor with hers so they wouldn't be sucked into the wormhole in the kitchen. She stared down at his face through the whipping curtain of her long hair. His blue eyes were still empty. Nothing she'd tried had gotten even a flicker of response from him.

She pressed her lips down on his slack mouth, kissing him as deeply and passionately as she could. Again there was no response.

"Max, please. Come back to me," she begged. "I love you so much, I don't even have the words to explain it. No one has invented the words for the way I love you. It would have to be some kind of chemical formula that would take a million blackboards or something."

Liz kissed him again. Then her mouth slipped. Her chin hit the floor. So did her body. Max—Max had disappeared, his molecules disbursing so quickly, Liz hadn't even been aware of it happening.

"Max," she cried. "Oh, Max, no!" She lifted her head and stared around the room as if she'd find him leaning up against one of the walls, smiling at her in that way that only Max had ever smiled at her, the way he never smiled at anyone *but* her. "Max!" she shouted again.

And in her mind his voice answered. "Even if my molecules were spread out from here to whatever galaxy my home planet is in, that wouldn't stop me. All my molecules would be like little homing pigeons. They'd all zoom to you, and then I'd re-form."

It was the voice of memory, something Max had said to her in a conversation long ago. Liz had told him his theory was romantic, but not scientific.

"But maybe that's what the love formula would be," she whispered. "Maybe love is the strongest bond between molecules, not something like shared electrons." She stretched her arms out in front of her and put her head down again, forced to keep her body flat so she wouldn't be pulled toward the hole. If she could somehow split her own body into molecules, maybe each of them could find one of Max's and bond with it. Even if she never got her body back, she'd be with Max. There was nothing more important than that.

But she wasn't an alien. She had no powers. She couldn't break herself into molecules without help.

I've got to try, she decided. She remembered how Max had discovered he could scatter his molecules. He'd been connected to the consciousness, and the beings had been exploring his memories. He'd said he'd felt like he was dissolving, and then it happened—his body had began to disappear as the molecules flew apart.

Liz conjured up the first memory that came to her—Max healing her. She envisioned throwing the memory out into the universe, as far away from her body as she could get it. Then she remembered kissing Rosa's cool cheek as she lay in her coffin, the smell of her sister's too heavy mortuary makeup strong in Liz's nostrils. She threw that out, too.

She didn't hold back anything. She had no shame. No pride. No secrets. She flung out the memory of getting her period for the first time—standing in the shower and thinking for a minute that she had some horrible disease and that a doctor was going to have to look at her down there. She flung out the memory of lying to her mama about stealing a little toy truck from a toy store when she was four. She let go of every thought she'd had about Max, good and bad. Every fantasy she'd had about him, even the ones she could hardly believe had come out of her own mind.

Liz released the memory of Maria's kitten scratching her lip when Liz was using a piece of string to play with it. She released the raw fury at her papa that she was shocked to find still had a place in her heart.

Her body began to feel lighter. She didn't lift her head to see if anything was happening. She kept calling up the memories, then letting them go. Calling them up, letting them go. Feeling the power of gravity release her. Feeling her heart stop beating. Feeling her lungs stop taking in air.

And then blackness.

And then silvery light.

Liz didn't even know how she was seeing the light. For she had no eyes. No body. No way to sense anything. But somehow she was experiencing silvery light.

The light shattered into silvery splinters, and Liz realized they were stars. She was surrounded by them.

Maybe we're the binary pair we saw that night out in the desert. Liz didn't know how she heard the words, any more than she knew how she was the stars. But she knew the words were from Max.

The closest star expanded and took on a new shape. Max. A shining silver Max. He reached out and touched her face with his glittery fingers, and she realized she did have a body after all, or at least she did now—a body like his, more glow than substance.

She pulled him to her, embraced him, never wanting to let him go. For an instant their bodies became one blinding star, then separated into the glowing forms again.

We need to get back. The others might need us, Max communicated soundlessly.

Liz laughed, feeling the laughter but not hearing it. *You're still Mr. Responsible. It's one—one of the many—things I love about you.*

Yeah, I know, Max communicated. *I know a lot of things now. We're going to have to . . . talk about those fantasies you've been having.*

Max took her hand. He pointed at a small blue ball far below them. Earth. Then Liz felt her molecules dissolve again, dissolve and mix with Max's.

"Oh, my God! Look!" Maria cried over the sound of the wormhole. "Am I seeing what I think I'm seeing?"

"Max!" Isabel exclaimed.

"I guess I am!" Maria shouted. This was . . . phenomenal. That was the only word for it. Max and Liz had teleported into the museum, arms wrapped around each other, looking so happy, so love struck, that they almost glowed. Without letting go of each other, they stumbled toward the wall where Maria and the others had strapped themselves. They squeezed in between Maria and Isabel.

Maria grabbed Liz around the waist and held on tight to keep her from being sucked into the hole. She snagged a piece of Max's shirt with her other hand, and he smiled at her, his eyes bright and alert and Max-ified.

"Hi, everyone," he yelled.

"You guys are late. We've pretty much done everything without you," Michael shouted. Even through the noise Maria could hear the raw relief in his voice.

"We're not going to be able to keep the hole open much longer," Trevor shouted.

Maria felt like Trevor had picked up a baseball bat and bashed her over the head with it. The joy at seeing Max back, whole and just *him*, gushed out of her like blood from a wound. She was still happy for him and Liz in an intellectual sort of way. Ecstatic, really, even though she couldn't feel the ecstasy right now.

How could she? Michael was going to leave. And any chance Maria had of ever experiencing that Max-and-Liz kind of love was going with him. Maria knew she'd never love anyone else the way she loved Michael. It was impossible.

"Isabel?" Trevor called out. "Are you coming?"

Isabel wrapped her arms tighter around Max, her fingers brushing Maria's.

"I can't," she answered. "My family is here. My whole family." She smiled at Maria. "I can't leave."

Trevor unfastened the straps holding him to the

wall. He wrapped one of them around his fist to keep him from flying into the wormhole immediately.

"Isabel, I . . . I'll come back. I don't know how long it will take, but I promise I will."

"Yeah," Michael shouted. He unfastened his straps and grabbed onto Trevor's shoulder. "Let's go!"

That's it? Maria thought. That's it? He said one word to all of us. One *yeah*. And that's it?

She knew she should feel angry. But she didn't feel anything. She was sure she'd never feel anything ever again. How could she? Her heart was broken.

THIRTEEN

Michael tightened his grip on Trevor's shoulder. This was it. He was going home. He was glad there wasn't time for a lot of good-bye bull. It wasn't as if Max wouldn't know that Michael was happy he made it out alive. He didn't have to make some speech. It wasn't as if Izzy wouldn't know that he'd think about her every day if he didn't say it. It wasn't as if Maria—

He didn't intend to do it, but Michael turned his head, wanting just one more look. His eyes met Maria's, and even though he hadn't touched her, hadn't gotten close to touching her, a connection formed between them instantly.

Images of Maria shot into him with the impact of bullets. Maria telling him how she loved lavender crayons when she was a little girl. Maria fiercely demanding that Trevor tell her what he'd done to her brother. Maria helping Michael move from one foster home to another, whether he wanted her to or not. Maria snorting soda out her nose during the part of *Evil Dead 2* where the guy breaks dishes over his own head. Maria crying while watching *Starman*. Maria being tortured by Elsevan DuPris. Maria asleep in the front seat of his car, raspberry lips gently parted.

They're all roots, Michael realized. Each memory of Maria was a root she'd put down in his body. He tried to turn his head, tried to break the connection that had begun when his eyes met hers. But he couldn't. The images rushed on, invading all his senses now. With the smell of her pillow. With the smell of her hair. With the sound of her ridiculous giggle. With the taste of icing licked off her finger. With the soft, wet heat of her mouth. With the strength of her arms when she pulled him to her and held him tight.

Using all his energy, Michael forced his eyes shut. But he could still see Maria looking at him. Maria looking at him as if he was her entire universe.

"Michael, what's wrong?" Trevor called.

Too many roots, he thought. If Michael left, all those roots would pull free, pulling pieces of him with them. There wouldn't be anything left but broken, useless chunks.

He opened his eyes and faced his brother. "I can't do it. I'm sorry."

Trevor stared at him a long moment, then nodded. "Nothing to be sorry about," he answered. He glanced at the wormhole. "It's about to close. I have to go. I wish I didn't, but—"

"They need you," Michael finished for him. He tried to hand his brother the Stone of Midnight, but Trevor pushed it away.

"You keep it," he said. He grabbed one of the loose straps and pushed it into Michael's hand. Michael tightened his fingers around it, then released his grip on his brother's shoulder.

Trevor turned to Isabel, smiled, then let go of his own strap. Instantly his feet flew off the ground. He raised his arms over his head in a gesture of triumph as he was pulled up into the wormhole, up, up, and then out of sight.

The hole closed behind him, the sudden change in pressure making Michael's ears pop. No one spoke for a moment, then everyone started jabbering at once. The words swirled around Michael—"How did you . . . ," "You were going to go . . . ," "Your molecules were. . . ." He ignored them. He let go of the strap, and in two long strides he was in front of Maria.

Her eyes were on her knotted safety harness. She didn't look up, although he was sure she knew he was there. "I guess it finally sank in that Max and Isabel are your family, too. I know that you and Trevor are brothers, and I'm sure you'll see him again, but Max and Isabel—"

Why was she babbling about Max and Isabel? Didn't she know why he stayed? Impatiently he pushed her hands away from the harness. He gave the molecules a hard *shove* with his mind, severing the straps. He expected her to hurl herself at him. But she didn't. She didn't even look at him.

Michael crouched down a little so he could peer

into her face. Her cheeks were streaked with tears, and he realized she was trembling. He did a fast aura check. There was joy in the sparkling blue, but uncertainty, too. Hope and doubt. And pain.

"It's okay. You got it off. Go say hi to Max," she said, still refusing to meet his gaze.

The idiot girl. She really didn't know why he'd stayed. And why should she? Michael asked himself. All he'd been doing lately was shoving her away.

"Maria," he said. He couldn't choke out another word. He pulled her to him, wrapping one hand in her silky, bouncy hair, locking her body to his with the other hand. And then he kissed her. God, it had been so long. How had he survived without this? Why had he ever tried? There couldn't be anything better than this.

Michael deepened the kiss. He'd never be able to get enough of her. Never. An involuntary groan escaped his lips when she pushed him away from her. "I want the words," she announced, meeting his gaze full on.

"The words," he repeated, trying to get his brain functioning again. How could she even form a sentence after that kiss?

"The words," Maria repeated.

"Think three," Isabel suggested. He'd almost forgotten there were other people in the room.

"Think something starting with an *l*," Alex added.

Heart pounding, Michael ran his fingers down Maria's cheek, wiping away some of the tears. Did she think he couldn't do this? Did she actually believe this would be hard?

"I love you." The words came out of his mouth like birds being freed from a cage. It felt so good, he said it again. "I love you, Maria."

The silver sparkles in her beautiful blue aura glittered like stars. "I love you, too."

"Did you see Michael's face?" Isabel asked Alex. "He actually didn't know what words she was talking about at first."

"Well, the guy is kind of dense," Alex answered.

"Unlike Max, who knew he loved Liz about one second after he saw her," Isabel said. She glanced over at her brother. Not that she could see much of him. He and Liz were wrapped around each other so tight, it was hard to tell where she ended and he began.

"Are you feeling a little . . . out of place?" Alex asked. He shook his head as he glanced from Michael and Maria to Max and Liz.

"I'm feeling a little lonely, if you want to know the truth," Isabel admitted. "When I saw Trevor disappear, it started up this, I don't know, this ache inside me."

Alex smoothed a section of her hair away from her face, then slid his arm around her shoulders. She leaned against him, letting his warmth seep into her.

"You've changed a lot, you know?" he asked, his breath tickling the top of her head.

"No, I haven't," she answered. "I was always this perfect."

Alex laughed. "Okay, yeah, you were. But you never would have admitted something like feeling lonely. That would have been too humiliating for Isabel Evans, the girl who didn't need anything from anybody."

"That's not true. I always needed things from people," Isabel protested.

"Of course you did. But you didn't admit it then. Now you do," Alex explained matter-of-factly.

He had her there. "Only to some people." Isabel twisted around so she could look him in the eyes. "People I know I can trust."

Alex nodded. "You're kind of dense yourself, you know," he told her. "It took you a while to figure out that you could trust me, if you'll remember. I'm glad you finally realized I'd do anything for you." He kissed her quickly, lightly.

"I know," Isabel answered. She really had been dense. There were so many times she'd treated Alex unfairly. So many times she'd accused him of things he wasn't close to being guilty of. And yet here he was. Right by her side.

"I'd do absolutely anything," Alex continued. "So if it gets close to your junior prom and you don't have a date, I'll try and squeeze you in. You know that I do have quite the social calendar going, and I—"

"Alex!" she squealed, whacking him on the head.

"It's hard to accept when the wheels of popularity turn, isn't it?" he asked, grinning. "One day you're up. The next day it's, um, let me see, that would be *me*. You're lucky I have a forgiving nature."

Isabel hugged him tightly and closed her eyes. "Very lucky," she agreed.

"Then your molecules . . ." Max kissed Liz's upper lip. "Just somehow went and found my molecules?" He kissed her lower lip. It had been so long. So, *so* long. Trapped at the bottom of the consciousness, the memory of Liz's touch had been all that kept him sane. All that kept him alive.

"I think so." Liz kissed the side of Max's neck. "Or maybe . . ." She kissed the little hollow at the base of his throat. "Maybe your molecules pulled mine to them. That's the more logical explanation." Her mouth returned to his, her tongue to his. He was home. He was really home.

Max pulled Liz closer against him, lifting her feet off the ground. She locked her legs around his waist, curling her fingers into his hair. "I'm never going to let anything come between us again. Never," he murmured against her lips, not wanting to lift his completely away from hers.

"There's definitely nothing coming between you right now," Alex called out. "You know you have a sister over here who might want to tell you she's glad you're still alive or something."

Max let Liz slide down his body to the ground. She started to step away, but he looped his arm around her waist. "You're not going anywhere," he told her as he reached for Isabel and pulled her into a hug with him and Liz. "Thanks for getting me back, Iz," he said, feeling her aura swirl through his. "I'm sorry about—"

"Oh, shut up," Isabel answered. "And you—," she called to Alex. "You get over here, Mr. Popularity." She grabbed his hand and tugged him toward her without letting go of Max.

Max grinned as he felt Alex's bright orange aura join the mix.

"Michael! Maria! Over here!" Isabel ordered with a laugh. "None of us really needs to see the two of you rolling around on the floor."

A moment later their auras joined Max, Liz, Alex, and Isabel's. A shimmering rainbow of color appeared around the six of them, the strands of jade green, warm amber, screaming orange, rich purple, bright blue, and brick red binding them together.

Max had never seen anything so beautiful in his life. He looked around at the faces of his closest friends—his family. The people that had saved his life. There was nothing he could use to describe this moment except full. Full of everything good and happy and pure.

"Remember?" Liz asked, looking each of them in the eye. Everyone smiled, clearly thinking about that first time they'd all connected, back when they'd needed to prove they could trust each other. It seemed so long ago, but it was the clearest memory in Max's mind.

He pulled Liz and Isabel a little bit closer and sighed with content. "How could any of us ever forget?"